Imperfect Love Story

Makiya Smith

Imperfect Love Story © 2016 by Makiya Smith

All rights reserved. Printed in the United States of America. No part of this book may be used or reproduced in any manner whatsoever without written permission except in the case of brief quotations embodied in critical articles or reviews.

This book is a work of fiction. Names, characters, businesses, organizations, places, events and incidents either are the product of the author's imagination or are used fictitiously. Any resemblance to actual persons, living or dead, events, or locales is entirely coincidental.

ISBN: 978-1537656618

CHAPTER 1

It was Nyshell's first day at her new school. She felt like she'd been there longer because she knew almost everyone. Nyshell was a junior in high school. She was seventeen years young with a banging body—a Coke-bottle shape. She was caramel skinned with really deep dimples and had almond-shaped eyes that gave her an innocent look. She was beautiful and shy.

Nyshell and her best friend, Breanna, were standing by the locker talking when their friend Justin walked up. Breanna and Nyshell has been best friends since they were six years old. They were complete opposites yet the same. Nyshell was shy and quiet, while Breanna was outspoken and not as quiet. Breanna was light skinned with dark brown eyes. She had lengthy hair, which was all natural, with the same body shape as Nyshell but smaller. They were both so silly. They were like two peas in a pod.

Justin, whom they'd known since middle school, was walking with some other dude.

He is so cute, Nyshell thought as she watched the dude who was with Justin. Justin was tall and had brown skin, really pretty teeth, and a nappy temp fade.

"What's good, y'all?" Justin gave Breanna and Nyshell a hug.

"Nothing, we're just waiting for the bell to ring." Breanna leaned back on the locker with her foot up, posing like a dope boy on the block.

Nyshell didn't know the dude was checking her out just as much as she was checking him out.

Justin, Breanna, and Nyshell joked around until the bell rung. All the while, the dude was watching Nyshell. He noticed how her smile was so adorable. He caught all her jokes and how silly she was. He was crushing. So was she.

"See you later, homie. Stay up. One love, my g." Nyshell pounded her chest with her fist like she saw in the movies. Breanna, Justin, and the dude laughed at her silliness. She laughed too.

"See you later, Shell!" Justin said as he and the dude walked off.

Nyshell watched the dude walk in the opposite way. He felt eyes on him, so he looked around and caught Nyshell staring. She hurried up and turned her head away, but it was too late. He caught her choosing. Nyshell was slightly embarrassed.

"Yo, Bre, who was dude rolling with Jus?" Nyshell asked Breanna.

"That's Drew Mason. Why, you want him?"

A smirk came across Nyshell's face, and Breanna knew then what was up.

"Want me to put in word to Justin?"

"Nah, but Imma catch you after class." Nyshell strolled to first period, which was chemistry. She walked into the classroom, went to the teacher's desk, and gave him her schedule.

"Hey, Ms. Robinson, you're late on your first day."

She peeped how the teacher tried making his seriousness a joke. "Sorry, I couldn't find your class," she quickly lied. Nyshell looked around and noticed a couple of people. She caught butterflies when she saw the dude, Drew. He flashed the prettiest smile she'd ever seen, and Nyshell felt like she was going to melt.

"Okay, take a seat next to Ms. Sheffield." It was a girl she knew from middle school, Lashay. Nyshell took a seat next to Lashay. The seat was right across from Drew's table. Lashay noticed how Nyshell and Drew were sneaking glances at each other.

"Y'all must like each other, girl?" Lashay whispered to Nyshell. She asked the question in a joking manner, but Nyshell wasn't cool with discussing that with her.

Instead of telling her, Nyshell simply replied, "Nah, I just think he's cute."

"Whew! Glad you said that." Lashay dramatically wiped her forehead.

"Why you say that?" Lashay now had Nyshell's undivided attention.

"Because he's a dog. He don't want nothing but what's between your legs. That boy belongs to the city." Nyshell didn't care though. She knew that there would be more people like Lashay. Instead of saying something back, she just gave a fake laugh and got back to her work.

First period went by, and Nyshell met Breanna at their locker. "Guess who is in my class, B?" Nyshell said as she approached Breanna.

"Who?"

"Drew, but you remember ol' girl Lashay?"

"Yeah, why? Wassup?" Breanna was skeptical.

"She's in there too. She told me he's a dog. He's for everybody."

"She told you she had sex with him?" Breanna crossed her arms.

"Nah, she ain't tell me that one." Nyshell shook her head. "Oh, so that's why she was bashing on him like that."

"Well, yeah. She thought that he was gonna make her his girl. Ever since then, she's been throwing salt on him."

"Females are crazy." They both laughed at Nyshell's comment.

"You wanna go to the football game this afternoon?" Breanna asked Nyshell.

"Yeah, that's cool."

Breanna and Nyshell headed to lunch. Nyshell couldn't stop thinking about Drew. She hadn't liked a boy since forever. She'd never been in a real relationship. Although she was only a junior, she still felt that she deserved a boyfriend—a good one at that. The boys she had come in contact with were lames. They were always flexing like they were getting paper or like they were messing with her a lot when knowing they only wanted one thing.

Breanna and Nyshell sat at the lunch table.

"I'm getting in line, you coming?" Breanna looked at Nyshell, who was looking around the cafeteria.

"Nah, Imma wait here."

Breanna walked to the line.

"Oh, you too good to eat school food?" Justin snuck up behind Nyshell.

She laughed at his smart comment. "Nah, I just don't mess around with that nasty stuff."

Justin sat next to her. "You know my boy like you?"

Nyshell decided to play dumb. "Who?"

"The boy who was walking with me earlier. His name is Drew."

Nyshell knew who he was talking about all along. "How you know?" She blushed.

"'Cause I know."

"I heard ya boy come with baggage."

"Who told you that?"

She didn't want to bust Lashay out, but she didn't want him to think she was lying. "Lashay."

"That broad just mad," Justin stated. Nyshell knew why he said that, but she kept quiet.

Breanna came back with her food. "What's good, Jus?"

"Nothing." He grabbed a chicken tender off her plate. So did Nyshell.

"Y'all should have got in line." Breanna snatched her plate away from Nyshell and Justin. They both laughed at her.

"Yo, chill. It ain't that deep." Justin teased Breanna. She flicked him her middle finger. "Ya girl like my boy though." Justin nodded his head toward Nyshell.

"She knows, honey." Nyshell playfully hit his arm. They sat at the table, talking and laughing, but Nyshell's mind was stuck on Drew.

Ding. Ding. It was the bell ringing for second period.

"Y'all come to the game this afternoon. Our school is playing at the stadium."

"Okay, we will," Nyshell spoke up for them both.

Breanna finished up her food, and she and Nyshell walked to their second period class: gym.

CHAPTER 2

Nyshell was at home, waiting for Breanna and her mom to pull up.

Honk. Honk.

Nyshell knew it was Breanna. She rushed out the house and locked the door. It was only a five-minute drive. They pulled up to the stadium in no time. Breanna's mom dropped them off and kept going.

As Nyshell and Breanna were paying for their tickets, Breanna felt her phone vibrate. She got it out of her pocket. It was a text message from Justin, saying that he was waiting for them by the entrance. "Justin said he's by the entrance," Breanna informed Nyshell after they got their tickets.

They walked in and spotted Justin waiting for them.

"We're sitting on this side. It's the first quarter," Justin told them as they walked with him.

Butterflies formed in Nyshell's stomach when she got to her seat. Drew was sitting there. *Justin knows what he's doing.* She tried playing cool, but her smile wouldn't go away.

"I'm the reason you smiling like that?" Drew was smiling also. His question made Nyshell blush.

"You can say that." She took a seat next to him.

They watched the game. Breanna noticed they were sneaking glances at each other. She was happy to see Nyshell crushing.

"Look at your girl." Justin slightly bowed Breanna to get her to look at Drew and Nyshell. She was getting some from Drew's head. Breanna smiled. Drew was right up Nyshell's alley. He was tall and chocolate and had a nice smile. She looks for that in boys.

Breanna and Justin continued watching the game while Nyshell and Drew watched each other.

"How are you getting home?" Drew asked Nyshell when the game was over.

"I'm riding with Breanna."

"Okay. Put your number in my phone." He handed Nyshell his phone.

"Put yours in my phone." She handed him her phone.

"This minicomputer," Drew cracked on Nyshell's big phone. They both laughed.

"Shut up talking about my phone. Here." She gave him his phone back, and he gave her hers.

"I'm gonna call you when I get to the spot?" Drew said more in a question than telling.

"Okay," Nyshell replied and started walking off.

"Dang, I can't get a hug?" Drew held his arms out.

"My bad." Nyshell slightly chuckled. She hugged him, and they went their separate ways.

Nyshell and Breanna walked to the gas station next to the stadium.

"I see you crushing on ol' boy hard," Breanna said to Nyshell in a teasing manner.

"Yeah, he's cool." Nyshell was nonchalant. They both burst into laughter, knowing it was more than just that.

"I saw you choosing," Breanna said with a smirk.

"I saw you see me choosing." They started laughing again.

"You really like him?" Breanna asked seriously.

"Yeah, I like his personality too. He so down to earth and nice."

"I'm happy that you're happy. Remember what we both said though."

"What?" Nyshell asked in confusion.

"'We will not look stupid for no boy or let a boy hurt us. If that boy doesn't do right—'"

"'Kick him to the curb,'" Nyshell finished as she remembered them both agreeing on those exact words.

"You remember?" Breanna asked Nyshell.

"Yeah, I remember, Bre. I got you," she said as Breanna's mom pulled up in front of them.

When she pulled up to Nyshell's house in Pittsburgh, where Nyshell lived with her mom and little sister, Breanna's mom said, "See you later, Shell. Love you."

"Love you too, Ma. See y'all later. Love you, B."

"Love you too. Imma hit your phone."

"'K." Nyshell checked around the house. Her mom and little sister were asleep. She jumped in the shower for fifteen minutes. The whole time she was in the shower, she thought about Drew. She imagined what it would feel like being his girl.

Right before Nyshell dozed off, her phone started to ring. It was Drew. "Wassup?" Nyshell asked.

"You ready to be my girl?" Drew got straight to the point.

"Yes!" Nyshell was smiling from ear to ear.

Just like that, they became a thing.

CHAPTER 3

It had been three months since the game and since Drew had made Nyshell his girl. She was finally getting to feel what a real relationship felt like. Drew would shower Nyshell with gifts and treat her like a queen. She felt like she'd found her Prince Charming. Girls around the school were jealous, but Nyshell didn't have a care in the world. She made sure everyone knew Drew belonged to her.

Drew and Nyshell were perfect for each other. The vibes were always good. They laughed and joked like friends, and there were rarely any arguments between the two because of all the silliness.

Drew Mason was the senior star basketball and baseball player. He was the shooting guard for basketball and pitcher for the baseball team. Drew was mostly known because of his good looks and good skills in sports. He'd been in sports since he was five. His number has always been fourteen; he chose his number because of his birthday being November 14th.

Nyshell was sitting in the living room watching television when Drew texted, *Get ready, I'm coming to take you out.* Nyshell was up and ready to go within ten minutes. She wore barely makeup with red MAC lipstick. Her Brazilian deep wave was down her back. She was wearing white highway jeans from H&M, a black crop top, and black Vans with spikes on the back. Her shape made the outfit even more pretty.

Knock. Knock. It was Drew at the door. Nyshell practically ran to answer it. Drew was taken aback when he saw Nyshell. Her outfit was pretty, but he didn't like the fact that her shirt barely covered her. He hugged her and kissed her.

"You got on that Thot top," Drew shaded Nyshell.

Her smile dropped because she was offended. "Whatever." She waved him off to get her jacket. Drew walked behind her and grabbed her butt. She tried taking his hands off but couldn't.

"You look so good we might not make it."

Nyshell played his comment off with a laugh. Drew had been bringing up sex a lot, but she insisted that she wasn't ready. "Let's go, Drew." She got away and walked toward the door. She turned around to see Drew fixing the bulge in his pants.

"This your fault." His eyes were bucked. Nyshell laughed at his facial expression. It was too cute.

On the way there, Nyshell and Drew learned more about each other. He learned that Nyshell's dad abandoned her when she was only one, cutting off all contacts with her mom and leaving them for good. Growing up, it had hurt and she had wished things were in her favor. She mentioned how they had seen her dad, but he had acted as if he didn't know them. She had gone home and cried her heart out, left wondering why he didn't want anything to do with her. Ever since then, she hadn't cared about his presence. Nyshell looked at it as his loss.

As Drew was driving, Nyshell checked him out. He looked so good to her. He was leaning back with his right hand on the steering wheel. He was wearing a black blazer, a black button down, and black fitted pants, all from Zara. He wore black Giuseppe sneakers that had silver zippers on them. He was pushing his mom's 2016 Camaro like a pro driver. Drew came from a family with money. His dad was an accountant for A-list celebrities and his mom was a travel agent with her own company.

Nyshell and Drew were at Ruth's Chris Steakhouse, sitting at a booth all the way in the back. "What should I get?" She was talking to herself more than she was to him as she bit on her bottom lip.

"Get whatever you want." Drew eyed her seductively.

Nyshell finally decided on what she was going to eat. She settled for their popular steak, which was what Drew ate also. She was scared to eat in front of him at first because she'd never been out like this. Drew noticed how she was trying to eat slow and cute at the same time. He chuckled a bit.

They enjoyed their meal and left. Drew wanted to stop at Cumberland mall, where he bought Nyshell Victoria Secret panties and a pair of shoes. They then stopped at the cookie stand.

"Nyshell, is that you?" It was Nyshell's ex, Kalon. Kalon was five nine with brown skin and a temp fade. He was wearing Jeremy Scott Adidas, black and white Adidas pants, and a white Ralph Lauren V-neck.

Damn, Nyshell thought. Kalon had always been fly, but he looked better than Nyshell remembered. She gave a shy smile.

"Hey, Kae." Nyshell hugged him.

"What's up? How you been?" Kalon looked Nyshell up and down. Drew walked in between them.

"Um," Drew cleared his throat, interrupting their conversation.

"Oh, Drew, this is—" Nyshell started to say but was cut off.

"I don't care to know. Let's go." Drew roughly grabbed Nyshell's arm, catching her off guard.

"Stop it, Drew. You're making a scene." Nyshell tried to get away as people watched the two. Kalon didn't say anything as he watched Drew practically drag Nyshell out the mall. "What

13

are you doing, Drew?" Nyshell yelled at him when they got in the car.

Drew had this crazed look in his eyes. He said nothing as he hit the steering wheel, causing Nyshell to jump. "Nyshell, don't you *ever* in your life disrespect me like that!" He gripped the steering wheel firmly. Nyshell said nothing out of fear. Drew pulled off and dropped Nyshell back home, neither one of them saying anything to each other.

The next day in class, Drew was already seated. Nyshell eyed the seat next to him and tried to decide whether or not she wanted to sit there. Drew could tell Nyshell was a bit shaken up about yesterday. She barely said anything throughout the whole day.

"I love you, Nyshell. I'm just afraid of losing you," Drew said before Nyshell got on the school bus to go home.

"I understand," Nyshell said.

"Let me take you out." He rubbed her hand, trying to butter her up. Nyshell fell for it. He took her out to eat, and just like that, Nyshell forgot yesterday even happened.

CHAPTER 4

"Wake up!" Nyshell's mom called out. It was 7:45. Nyshell was exhausted, and her mom could tell. She had stayed up all night on the phone with Drew.

"You should've gone to sleep early instead of staying up all night with Drew." Her mom gave her the side eye. She didn't mind because Nyshell was older; she had been there before herself.

Nyshell slowly crawled out of bed, grabbed her phone, and headed to the kitchen. Nyshell walked into the kitchen, smiling and blushing at her phone as she read the text: *Good morning, beautiful, can't wait to see you.*

"That boy must really got your head gone?" Nyshell's mom interrupted.

"Huh?" Nyshell gave a puzzled look.

"Huh nothing." Her mom's tone dripped with sarcasm.

"Yeah, I mean, I like him a lot, I guess." Nyshell felt like a window standing there in front of her mom.

"Oh yeah? So, when am I going to meet him?"

"Meet him?" Nyshell spit out the water.

"Something wrong with your ears this morning? Yes, meet him. I'm not going to scare him off." Nyshell knew her mother wasn't going to do anything to jeopardize their relationship,

15

she just didn't know how Drew would feel about meeting her mother after only three months. She still decided to ask him about it. "Ummm, soon," Nyshell said hesitantly.

"I sure do hope soon means soon. Hurry and eat up before you miss your bus. I have to go. Love you."

"Love you more!" She gave her mom a hug.

All Nyshell could think about was her mom meeting Drew. *What would she think of him? What would happen? What would Drew think?* All the possibilities and scenarios were just running through her mind.

That same morning, she was at the locker early, waiting for Breanna. As soon as Breanna walked up, Nyshell told her that her mom wanted to meet Drew.

Breanna knew it was a big deal and was just as nervous as Nyshell, but someone had to be the sane one. "Ny, calm down. It's not that big of a deal. She'll love him," Breanna said, trying to bring Nyshell back to earth.

"But what if she doesn't?"

"Stop, you're only scaring yourself."

"You know what, you're right. I'm going to talk to Drew about it in first period," Nyshell said, hoping that first period would be delayed. Time must've not been on her side because as soon as she said it, the bell rang.

"See you later, Shell, and don't be nervous—just ask," Breanna said as the two parted ways.

Nyshell's walk to first period felt shorter than usual. She walked in first period just as everyone else was coming in. She took her seat next to Drew after she hugged him and gave him a peck on the cheek.

"Dang, I get a kiss on the cheek? I couldn't wait to see you, but you're making me reconsider." Drew said jokingly.

Nyshell chuckled, "I couldn't wait to see you either."

"Then show me." Drew eyed Nyshell like she was a piece of candy. Nyshell leaned over, and they started tonguing each other down.

"No, this is not the place! Warm up is on the board," Mr. Hall chimed in as he pointed to the board.

"See, you got me in trouble," Nyshell said, pushing Drew away.

"So? He's just jealous," Drew said with a wink, causing Nyshell to blush. They started their warm up, and Nyshell finished first, as always. Usually, she'd help Drew or compare their answers, but today she just stared off into space, playing with her pen and thinking about how he would react.

"What's wrong?" Drew asked, studying Nyshell.

"Nothing, what do you mean?" Nyshell answered.

"Nyshell, I know you, and I know when something's wrong."

"Okay. My mom asked about meeting you, and I'm not sure if you would want to," Nyshell confessed truthfully but quickly.

"That's what you're worried about?" Drew asked, looking at her like she had sprouted three heads.

"Yes, what if it doesn't go well?" Nyshell shot back, giving him the same facial expression.

"Stop worrying so much. It will. Just let me know when. She'll love me," Drew said confidently.

"How about tomorrow night?"

"Okay!"

Nyshell quickly shot her mom a text: *Drew is coming over tomorrow night.*

***

It was the night Drew and her mom were supposed to meet, and Nyshell didn't realize that she would be this nervous. Her mom was in the kitchen, cooking, while Nyshell went back and forth from the living room and kitchen, texting Breanna and trying to make sure everything was perfect.

Ding dong. The doorbell rang.

"It's Drew!" Nyshell joyfully hollered.

"I'll get it. You go butter the biscuits," Nyshell's mom said.

Nyshell's face dropped, wondering why her mom wouldn't let her get the door. Her mother saw her reaction and laughed. "Ma, you know you wrong," Nyshell said seriously.

"Baby, eventually you'll learn that it's all about strategy. If he sees you in the kitchen, he'll think you can cook," her mom said jokingly, causing them both to laugh—they both knew that Nyshell could burn water.

Nyshell headed for the kitchen as her mom opened the door for Drew. Nyshell's mom had to admit her daughter has taste. He was good looking, looked her in the eyes as he confidently spoke, and, as far as she knew, played sports.

"Come on to the kitchen. Dinner is just about ready," Nyshell's mom said as she guided Drew to the kitchen.

"I hope it tastes as good as it smells," Drew said, trying to butter Nyshell's mom up.

"Trust me, it tastes better," she replied confidently. Nyshell's mom laughed when she walked in and saw that Nyshell had on an apron, knowing that she had taken her advice. Nyshell and her mom put the finishing touches to the food as Drew stood back and watched.

Just as they were about to take the food into the dining area, Drew spoke up, "I'll set the table."

"You don't have to," Nyshell said quickly.

"It's the least I can do," Drew said as he flashed his beautiful smile.

"Plates are in the cabinets." Nyshell's mom pointed to the cabinet above the microwave. Drew got the plates and went in the dining room to set the table. Nyshell's mom was surprised when she walked in and everything was set up as if she had done it herself. They all had just sat down to eat when Nyshell's little sister, Nya, started crying, waking up from her nap.

"I guess someone else is hungry too," Nyshell's mom said, referring to Nya.

As soon as her mom got up, Nyshell asked Drew, "What did my mom say to you when she opened the door?"

"Mind your business," Drew said, laughing at Nyshell's nosiness.

"Whatever, Drew!" Nyshell said, throwing a napkin at him.

"You look good, baby. If your mama wasn't here, I'd be all over you," Drew said, biting his lip. Nyshell was a virgin, but Drew knew just what to say to make her want to know what it felt like to not be one.

When Nyshell's mom returned, she had Nya in her arms. Nya stared at Drew. Drew just smiled and then waved at her until she finally waved. After she waved back, Nya was cool with him, trying to talk and smile with him all night.

"I see you've won somebody over," Nyshell's mom said as she and Drew laughed.

Over dinner, as everyone talked, Nyshell was still nervous and scared that someone might say the wrong thing. Nyshell eventually lightened up because she knew that the laughs meant he had won her mom over too.

When dinner was over, Drew helped with the dishes while Nyshell went to her room. Nyshell texted Breanna to let her know that everything went well. Drew and her mom made more small talk until they were done. Drew then went to Nyshell's room until they heard his mom beep the horn to pick him back up. Nyshell walked him to the door, and they kissed and said their goodbyes.

"Lock the door. Love you. I'll text you when I get home." Drew turned to walk away.

"Okay, love you too." Nyshell closed the door and leaned against it, feeling that mushy feeling in her heart. She loved Drew so much. She went to the bathroom, where her mom was bathing her little sister. "So, what do you think of him.?" Nyshell nervously asked, wanting the truth.

"He aight. I mean, whatever," her mom said jokingly. They both started laughing.

Ever since dinner that night, Drew had been coming over a couple of times a week and their relationship was stronger than ever.

One Sunday afternoon, Drew came over when Nyshell's mom and little sister were gone. Nyshell and Drew were watching Netflix and chilling. She was nervous because the night before they had been talking about sex. It was something Drew had begun to bring up a lot all of a sudden. He would ask and ask. He had put her in a situation where she'd felt obligated, but she'd said nothing and was cool with it. She wanted to know what it felt like.

Now here she was, lying beneath him with her shirt halfway up. He was kissing all over her and rubbing on her body. Although it felt good, her mind was in another place. It felt like her heart was in her stomach and she had the bubble guts. She wanted so bad to say, "Stop," but she was scared he'd get mad. She was stuck between a rock and a hard place.

Nyshell began to think about Lashay. She wanted so bad to know why there was bad blood between the two and if it were something he had done. "Drew, can I ask you something?" Nyshell softly spoke up.

"Ask." Drew was deep in the moment.

"What happened with you and Lashay?" Nyshell nervously asked, not wanting to kill the vibe, but that was exactly what she did.

"We messed around, but she tried to make it seem as if I dogged her out. Sex was all it was. Nothing more, nothing less," Drew explained truthfully as he sat straight up on the bed.

"I don't want to be like—"

"YOU'LL NEVER BE LIKE HER! You're my girl, Nyshell. It'll never be just sex between us," Drew angrily cut her off.

"I didn't mean to make you upset," Nyshell timidly stated. "Let's just try sex another time. I'm not ready now."

"So why did you agree to it in the first place?" Drew voice boomed, scaring Nyshell. She didn't say anything. Instead, she just looked at him.

"Whatever, I'm ready to go." Drew got up and walked out of the house, calling his mom to come pick him up.

Nyshell came behind him, trying to apologize, but he told her to go back in the house. Even though she felt like he was hurt, she was hurt. She didn't feel like she had done anything wrong by asking him a question or telling him to wait for sex. Nyshell then started to feel bad for rescheduling their sex appointment when she was the one who agreed to it in the first place.

When she looked out the window ten minutes later, he was gone. They texted later that night, and he apologized for overreacting. The next day, Drew brought her flowers and they were hugged up at school as always, like the argument had never happened.

CHAPTER 5

Weeks had gone by since the night Drew had come over to Nyshell's house. Afraid of making him mad, Nyshell would come up with legit excuses to avoid them being alone. But Drew had caught on, so he figured he'd beat her at her own game. One Saturday, Drew just popped up. The day before, Nyshell had told him her mom and little sister would be gone and she was going over to Breanna's. He asked Breanna if Nyshell was over her house and took this opportunity to catch Nyshell before she left.

Knock. Knock. Nyshell was putting the finishing touches on her makeup but was startled when she heard the knock at the door. "Who is it?" Nyshell called out.

"Drew," he answered.

Nyshell was hesitant. "C—coming," she stuttered. Nyshell opened the door.

"What's good? You looking all pretty. Who you getting all dolled up for?" Drew sloppily kissed Nyshell. His vibe was off, and she could tell. It made her edgy. Drew could also tell Nyshell was nervous, but he wanted her that way. He didn't mention that he knew she was dodging him on purpose.

Nyshell tried downplaying the feeling.

"What's up? I missed you." He started kissing on her neck, placing patch marks on her purposely.

"Drewww," Nyshell whined, trying to break loose, but he was being really rough. He pulled her skirt up, and Nyshell froze. Drew stopped and studied her. She looked like a deer caught in the headlights. Drew burst into laughter, causing Nyshell to be confused. He pulled her skirt down and gave her a hug. She didn't know what to expect. In fact, she wanted to cry for help.

"I'm just playing. Where you headed?" Drew asked, as if he wasn't just about to be become a rapist.

It was awkward, weird, and very uncomfortable for Nyshell. "Breanna's house," Nyshell spoke up.

"Cool. I'll catch you later. Love you." Drew left, leaving Nyshell standing there.

No lie, Nyshell had to be standing there for about ten minutes. She didn't know what to do. She went upstairs to gather her things. As she was cutting her lights off, her phone beeped. It was a text message from Drew: *Don't tell anyone about what just happened.* Nyshell replied: *Don't worry, I won't!*

About ten minutes after that, he was texting her, telling her how sorry he was, he loved her, and he was out of his head. Just like that, she believed and forgave him.

The next day at school, when Nyshell got to her locker, Breanna was holding balloons and a card.

"Who's crushing on you?" Nyshell asked.

"These aren't for me. Drew left them for you," Breanna stated.

"Aww, he's so sweet," Nyshell said with a huge smile.

"What's the special occasion?" Justin asked sarcastically as he walked up.

"You know it doesn't have to be a special occasion when Drew's your man," Breanna stated jokingly as the three started laughing.

"Whatever, I'll see y'all later," Nyshell said as she was walking off, still smiling from the gifts. Her smile quickly turned into a frown when she saw Drew wasn't in first period. He was always in first period before her, but she just brushed it off. She finally decided to read the card. *Good morning! Sorry about what happened yesterday. Hope I can make it up to you. I'll be at your house later on. Love, Drew.* She was smiling so hard from the card she didn't realize Drew had walked in.

"I see you like my little apology," Drew said with confidence.

"Yes," she said, smiling.

"Shell, it won't happen again," Drew said, looking into her eyes. She started to think he really meant it and felt sorry for being scared of him.

That afternoon, Drew caught the school bus home with her. Shell's mom wasn't there. She had told Nyshell that she was working late. When Nyshell and Drew got to the house, they put their stuff in her room and headed for the kitchen. They both ate a hot pocket and a bag of chips.

When they were done, they went into her room and flipped through the channels. Nothing was on, so Drew decided they should just cut the TV off and talk. Nyshell was hesitant because with no one home, she knew what the talking would lead to. For some reason, this time she felt different about the topic. She felt like if she didn't do it, someone else would. She knew girls threw themselves at him. Also, she felt like their relationship was ready for it.

"Shell, why are you so quiet?" Drew asked.

"I'm just thinking," Nyshell said, knowing Drew wasn't going to just brush it off.

Just as she figured, Drew asked her, "About what?"

"Us and sex," she answered, trying not to make eye contact. Drew was lying across the bed, but he sat up when Nyshell mentioned sex. "I think I'm ready for it. And I think it'll be good for our relationship," Nyshell said.

"Are you sure?" Drew asked, acting like he was hesitant about it.

Nyshell's mind wasn't sure, but her mouth said, "Yes." Nyshell sighed.

"Yes" was all that Drew needed to hear.

She hadn't said anything but a word—literally. Next thing Nyshell knew, Drew was on top of her and they were kissing. Before she knew it, her and Drew's pants were off. Everything was happening so fast, and Nyshell didn't even realize what was going on or what was supposed to be happening. She had never been this close to sex, and it was weird for her. She wanted to tell Drew to stop, but she didn't want to disappoint him because she was the one who had brought up the subject.

When Drew pulled out his business, he stopped. Nyshell thought that Drew had realized she was uncomfortable, but he only stopped to pull out a gold magnum wrapper. In Nyshell's mind, she knew there was no turning back. She knew that "it" was about to happen. She was so deep in her thoughts that she wasn't paying any attention to Drew kissing her neck. The big question in her mind was *Why does Drew already have a condom?* This made the moment feel even less special to Nyshell, but she said nothing. She felt like Drew had known it was going to happen.

Nyshell's thoughts were erased when all she felt was pain coming from in between her legs. She quickly jumped up, but Drew told her to relax. She laid back down, putting her hands on his chest to keep him from going any further. Drew repeatedly told Nyshell to stop as he continued. Nyshell was gasping for air as Drew consistently penetrated her. Eventually, the pain stopped and all Nyshell felt was pleasure. Once Drew was done, he continued to kiss on Nyshell, which made her feel special.

When it was time for him to leave, neither of them wanted him to go. Drew was jumping for joy inside. He didn't call or text Nyshell that night, but she didn't pay it attention. She called Breanna and told her about it.

CHAPTER 6

It had been two weeks since Nyshell and Drew had had sex. Nyshell felt like everything was perfect and even better since they were now sexually active. She didn't notice Drew had stopped texting her in the morning. They also weren't texting the entire day anymore. She brushed it off as them being too used to each other . . . until one day when they were at her house.

Drew went to the bathroom, and she decided to look through his phone. Usually, she wouldn't have peeked through his phone, but she had the opportunity and took it. What she saw shocked her. Drew and his ex Keyanna had been texting back and forth. Drew was saying things that somebody in a relationship shouldn't be saying. When Drew came back from the bathroom, Nyshell still had his phone in her hand. She didn't try to hide the fact that she went through it. She could tell by the look in his eyes that he knew he'd been caught.

"Nyshell, give me my phone," Drew demanded.

"Yeah, you can have your phone—so you can text your lil girlfriend!" Nyshell shot back as she threw the phone to him.

"Calm down, 'cause it's not even like that," Drew tried to explain.

"Calm down? It's not like what? 'Cause last time I checked, if you're in a relationship, you don't call other girls 'baby.' Oh, you can't wait to see her? Bye, Drew," Nyshell said seriously.

"So, you're just going to let this girl ruin us? She don't mean anything. I just gave her a little conversation, that's all." Drew was trying to explain himself, but Nyshell wasn't having it. She was more upset at who the girl was whom he was still in love with.

Seeing those messages made Nyshell skeptical on whether or not he really loved her. She wasn't even sure if Drew really wanted to be with her. Those messages changed Nyshell's whole mindset about Drew. Drew was in the room, pleading for her forgiveness, but after a while, he just brushed it off, telling her she was either going to accept it or not. Nyshell told him that she didn't accept it, causing Drew to storm out. She thought he was just leaving the room to get some space until she heard the front door slam.

Nyshell jumped out of her bed and stormed after him. By the time she reached the front porch, Drew was walking down the end of the driveway. "Where are you going?" Nyshell yelled.

"Home!" Drew responded with an attitude.

"How?" Nyshell yelled back, but Drew continued to walk and ignore her. Drew's mom wasn't outside, and he didn't live in the neighborhood, so she followed him as far as she could until she had to return home. Her little sister, Nya, was in the house sleep, and Nyshell couldn't leave her alone. Once Nyshell was back in the house, she called Drew's mom to tell her that Drew was upset and walking down the street. His mother called Nyshell twenty minutes later, saying she had picked Drew up. Nyshell was relieved that Drew was somewhere safe, but she didn't know if they were together or not. She didn't really want to break up; she just didn't want to be the stupid girl who always forgave him.

Nyshell didn't know what to do, so she called Breanna. Once she told Breanna what had happened, Breanna was on the way. Breanna always had her back. She was her comfort, no matter what. When Breanna arrived, they went over every single detail. Breanna wanted to call and curse Drew out, but Nyshell wouldn't let her. Nyshell felt bad enough already that she'd made him mad enough to leave, but Breanna told Nyshell that it wasn't her fault. Nyshell was crying steadily. She was so in love with Drew that it made Breanna sick. Breanna was starting to dislike Drew more and more. But since Nyshell loved him, Breanna decided to not say anything for now.

"So, what's up with you and Drew now?" Breanna sincerely asked.

Nyshell shrugged her shoulders, letting Breanna know that she wasn't sure.

Breanna, Nya, and Nyshell chilled for the rest of the day until Breanna's mom came and got her. Nyshell checked her phone throughout the day, hoping that Drew had texted, but he never did. When eleven o'clock hit, she finally received a text from Drew. He was apologizing, telling her it'll never happen again. Young and in love, she forgave him.

CHAPTER 7

Nyshell was at Drew's house for the weekend. Her mom had dropped her off. They were getting ready to go to the movies. The movie *The Conjuring* had come out, and Nyshell wanted to see it, so Drew was making it a date.

Nyshell was in Drew's room getting dressed while he sat in the living room watching TV. He was giving her some privacy. "Drew!" Nyshell called out his name.

He got up and went to his bedroom. "Yes?" Drew answered as he admired her. She was wearing a black fitted dress with black boots, and her hair was already wand curled. He stood there, staring at Nyshell.

"What, Drew?" she asked, trying her hardest not to smile.

"You so beautiful." He winked at her, causing her to smile and then laugh.

"Thank you." She winked back, making him smile and laugh.

He walked over to her and kissed her on the forehead. She was blushing. "You ready? My mom gonna drop us off," Drew informed Nyshell.

"Yes, and okay. Let me grab my purse. I'll meet you downstairs," Nyshell told Drew.

33

He nodded and went downstairs. His mom was grabbing her things and wearing dark shades. "You ready, Ma?" Drew asked, scaring her and causing her to jump.

"You scared me, baby," she exclaimed with her hand over her chest. She laughed a little.

"I'm sorry, Ma." He leaned over to kiss her, and she jumped. Drew leaned back and studied his mom. She put her head down, feeling transparent in front of her own son.

"Where's Nyshell?" she asked, purposely keeping the attention off of herself.

"Here I am, Miss Claudia." Nyshell walked in the living room.

"Hey, girl, and I told you to call me 'Ma.' I ain't old enough to be called 'Miss,'" Drew's mom joked. The girls laughed. Drew was still stuck on his mom and the shades.

"Come on, y'all." Claudia grabbed her keys, and they hopped in the car.

Nyshell noticed how Drew was distant the whole ride. When she reached for his hand, he pushed it away.

"What movie are y'all going to see?" Claudia asked. Drew didn't say anything.

"We're going to see *The Conjuring*," Nyshell answered.

"Is that the scary movie?" she asked.

"Yes," Nyshell answered again.

"I don't see how y'all do those scary movies. I don't like them at *all*."

Drew was still quiet. Claudia knew how stubborn her son could be, so she decided not to say anything to him. She pulled up beside the curb. Drew hopped out and kept walking toward the movie theater.

"What's up with him?" Nyshell asked his mom.

"Just his temper. He'll be fine. You guys enjoy tonight. I'll be back," his mom replied, not wanting to tell why he was upset. Nyshell got out of the car, and Claudia pulled off.

"Drew!" Nyshell called after him, but he kept walking. Nyshell's phone started ringing. It was Breanna. "Hey, Bre," Nyshell answered her phone.

"I see you," Breanna teased.

"Really?" Nyshell got excited about Breanna being there.

"If this is you with the black dress, then, yes, I do," Breanna joked. They both laughed.

"Stop playing and come to me," Nyshell said, growing tired of playing.

Drew was watching her smile, and it made him jealous. He had no clue who she was talking to.

"Turn around. I'm across the street," Breanna told Nyshell. Nyshell did so as Breanna walked across the street.

"Hey, girl, where's Drew?" Breanna asked.

"He right—" Nyshell stopped when she saw Drew talking to a girl. They were both smiling.

"That's Keyanna. She went to school with me. They used to go out," Breanna informed Nyshell.

"He wouldn't even talk to me just now though." Nyshell's feelings were hurt.

"Come on." Breanna grabbed Nyshell and walked toward the two.

"Hey, Drew, here's your girlfriend." Breanna nudged Nyshell toward Drew. Keyanna laughed sarcastically.

"Whatever. I'll text you, Drew," Keyanna said and walked off.

"Yeah, whatever." Nyshell sized Keyanna up.

"Chill, man," Drew said to Nyshell.

"What you mean 'chill'? What she gonna text you for? You wouldn't even talk to me, but you all in her face, smiling like

I'm not here!" Nyshell yelled at Drew. People watched the two as they walked by. Drew hated people being in his business, and he wasn't feeling Nyshell talking to him like that.

"Go hang with Breanna or something. I'm not tryna hear all that right now," Drew dismissed Nyshell and she stood there, feeling dumb that he would dis her when she wasn't the one being disrespectful.

"Let's go," Nyshell said to Breanna. Her heart felt as if it were gonna explode. Nyshell and Breanna walked away from the movie theater.

"Look." Breanna pointed to Dejuan. He was rolling with Lando. Lando and Breanna secretly crushed on each other, but they were both scared to speak up.

Dejuan was from New Orleans. He was five eleven, brown skinned, and built. He was bowleg and always in the latest gear. Dejuan reminds you of Jim Jones. He was cool and laid back. Nyshell lived on the street he hung on and had crushed on Dejuan for so long. He secretly crushed on her also. They would speak every now and then but nothing ever serious. Nyshell was afraid of rejection, so she never had any intentions of expressing her feelings toward him.

Dejuan noticed Nyshell looking, so he approached her. "Hey, beautiful," he complimented Nyshell, making her blush.

"You hit all girls with that?" She played hard.

"Nope, all girls aren't you," Dejuan said back in his thick New Orleans accent.

"Whatever." Nyshell playfully gave him the hand.

"Let's go see a movie," Dejuan suggested.

Nyshell was nervous she'd see Drew, but then again, she figured he went in there with his ex, thinking Nyshell and Breanna had left. "It's on you?" Nyshell joked with the intentions of paying her own way.

"Let's have us a double date." Dejuan winked at both Nyshell and Breanna.

"Oh, you got jokes, Kevin Hart?" Breanna said as she laughed at Dejuan. The group laughed.

"Call it what you want. You know my boy like you. Stop playing him," Dejuan stated.

"Go head on, man." Lando slightly laughed. Lando was the same height as Dejuan but light skinned with green eyes and a curly temp fade. He was wearing black Timbs, a leather jacket with zippers, a beige Armani Exchange tee, and black Diesel jeans. Lando was from East Atlanta. Lando and Dejuan were first cousins and both went to school with Nyshell and Breanna.

They all walked in the movies. Lando paid for himself and Breanna, while Dejuan paid for himself and Nyshell. When they got inside, the previews were playing. Nyshell wanted to sit at the top, so they got seats in the top row. The boys sat on the outside of the girls.

"You wanted something from the concession stand?" Dejuan asked Nyshell when they got settled in their seats.

"Yeah, I thought the movie had started. I'll go in a minute," Nyshell whispered.

"I'll go. What you want from there?" Dejuan asked her.

"Nachos and a slushy. Here," Nyshell reached in her purse for her money.

"Nah, baby, keep your money." Dejuan pushed the money back toward her. Dejuan asked Lando to walk with him.

"Yeah, you want something?" Lando turned toward Breanna.

"Popcorn and a slushy," she replied.

"Cool." Lando and Dejuan jetted off.

When they were walking out, Drew was coming in with his ex behind them. Dejuan was confused. He thought Drew and Nyshell were dating.

Nyshell and Breanna were watching previews when they saw Drew walk in with his ex. Nyshell's eyes almost popped out of her head. Drew didn't even know she was watching. He had popcorn with the biggest cup of slushy from the concession stand in his hands. They sat four rows in front of Nyshell.

"Are you going to say anything?" Breanna asked Nyshell.

It was obvious that Nyshell was hurt. It showed all over her face. "Nah, I'm going to play back with him." Nyshell tried playing it off as if she wasn't hurt. She pulled out her phone and texted Drew, asking him where he was. He replied: *At home.* Nyshell couldn't help but laugh.

"He's a big liar." Breanna was growing angry as she watched Nyshell and Drew's messages.

Nyshell texted back, saying, *Oh, Bre said she thought she saw you in the movies.*

"*Lol, nah. I'm at home and I'm sorry about what happened. Love you! I'll text you when I wake up,*" Nyshell read aloud. She watched Drew put his phone in his pocket and put his arm around the girl. "He thinks *he's* the player." Nyshell got up and Breanna followed. "I thought you were at home." Nyshell approached Drew.

He looked as if he'd seen a ghost. "I . . . I can explain," he stuttered.

"Nah, you ain't got to. Do you!" Nyshell picked up his slushy and threw it in his face. It splashed on him and Keyanna.

"Yo, Nyshell!" Drew exclaimed.

Keyanna charged at Nyshell, and Nyshell punched her right over the seat. Drew grabbed Nyshell's neck, and Breanna grabbed his hand. As if on cue, Dejuan and Lando walked in. They both dropped their snacks and got Drew off of Nyshell. Luckily, the other people in the theater didn't call security just yet. Lando was holding Keyanna.

"Let her go!" Dejuan grabbed Drew.

Drew squeezed Nyshell's neck one last time and let go right when Breanna punched him in the face. Nyshell could barely breathe. She fell to the floor, coughing and trying to catch her breath. The security came, flashing their lights.

"What's going on here?" It was a Caucasian male. He flashed his light to Drew and saw that his white shirt was now red and blue and his lip was bleeding. There was slushy dripping all over his face. "You all have to go now," the security officer said firmly.

By now, Nyshell was getting off of the floor and dusting herself off.

"You good, li mama?" Dejuan hurried to her side. "Come on." He walked Nyshell out.

"Ahh haa!" Breanna stuck her tongue out at Drew's ex.

Drew rushed to Keyanna. She was yelling, screaming, and trying to get at Nyshell. She cursed at Breanna. She even cursed at Lando for holding her back. Nyshell, Dejuan, Lando, and Breanna all walked out as if nothing had happened.

Nyshell was blowed, hurt, and confused. All she could ask herself was *Where did I go wrong?* She had kept it real with Drew since they had become a thing. How could he lie to her like that? She couldn't think straight.

"I'm sorry about that, Ny. I shouldn't have left you back there," Dejuan apologized.

"It's okay. It wasn't your fault, Dejuan," Nyshell said as she held back tears.

"Come here." Dejuan held his hand out. "Your neck is messed up, baby." He tried lifting her neck up.

"Ouch!" Nyshell jumped.

"I should've blacked his eye!" Breanna said when she saw Nyshell's neck. It was purple. Drew's handprint could be seen, and there were scratches making her neck red as well.

"Damn, he messed ya neck up. Get in the car," Dejuan said. He was driving in a white Mustang. He unlocked the door and opened it for Nyshell. Lando and Breanna hopped in the back. Nyshell was deep in thought the whole ride, so she didn't say much.

"You want something to eat?" Dejuan looked over at Nyshell.

"No, I don't have an appetite," Nyshell said honestly.

"You got to eat, lil mama," Dejuan protested.

Nyshell knew he was right, but her mind wasn't even on food. She just wanted to run and hide from the humiliation. She felt so stupid. The feelings she had for Drew were so deep, but he still played her, as if she meant nothing to him. The crazy thing was she still wanted to be with him. "I'll eat in the morning. Right now, I want to rest. We're going to Breanna's house." Nyshell rested her head on her knuckles as she stared out the window.

Dejuan let it go. "Here," Dejuan handed Nyshell a $50 bill as he slowed in front of Breanna's driveway.

"What's this for?" Nyshell asked, confused.

"Get you something to eat." Dejuan motioned for her to take it.

Reluctantly, Nyshell grabbed the money.

"I'll see you later. Get some rest," he told her.

Lando hopped in the front. "Bre, hit my phone," Lando said to Breanna. She nodded, and Dejuan and Lando watched them walk in the house.

CHAPTER 8

Nyshell still hadn't talked to Drew—it had been two weeks, but she refused to give up that quick. He didn't even try to talk to her. That made her wonder. She was still hurting, and he didn't even care to talk things out.

In first period, he had changed his seat and talked to everyone but her.

Nyshell was walking to the restroom and happened to bump into Drew. He had just gotten to school. Drew was watching Nyshell. She acted as if she didn't see him and kept walking to the restroom.

"Nyshell?" Drew spoke up. Nyshell ignored him. "I'm sorry, Nyshell," he confessed. She still ignored him, which made him angry. He caught up with Nyshell and snatched her arm, slamming her to the wall. "Don't you hear me talking to you?" He jacked her shirt up.

Nyshell was totally caught off guard. "Scared" wasn't even the word to describe how she was feeling. She almost went right there in the hallway. "Let me go, Drew!" Nyshell tried getting away, but he had her pushed against the wall.

"You think you could get away with being at the movies with Dejuan?" He gritted through his teeth.

"No," Nyshell admitted.

"Okay then. I said I was sorry. Now you're going to forgive me," Drew demanded.

Nyshell didn't say anything. This wasn't the Drew she remembered. She didn't know the person standing there and demanding forgiveness when he was in the wrong.

"You hear me?" He jacked on her shirt.

"Yeah, Drew."

Drew eyed Nyshell one last time and let her fall to the floor. She just sat there and watched him walk away.

He stopped and turned around. "Get off the floor and come to class." He continued to walk.

Nyshell got up, dusted herself off, and walked to class. It seemed like the whole class was watching her. She walked to a seat in the back. For the rest of the class period, Nyshell said nothing. Drew would turn around and look at her every now and then, but she didn't pay him any attention.

School went by in a daze for Nyshell. She was quiet the whole day. Breanna was worried about her friend. It wasn't like Nyshell to be quiet for such a long period of time.

At the end of the day, Nyshell would post up outside, but not today. She hopped on the school bus and went home. Her heart was aching like never before. She put earphones in and listened to music the whole ride home.

"Have a good day," the bus driver said to the students who got off along with Nyshell.

Nyshell walked in the house. Her mom and baby sister wasn't there. She felt kind of relieved. She wanted to be alone. Alone. Serenity. Peace. She meandered around the house until she stumbled upon her bedroom doorway. Her legs gave way, and she fell on the bed. She couldn't stop replaying the events of the rough day over in her head. She wasn't hurt physically; she was hurt emotionally and feeling lost. She was crushed by a boy she was deeply in love with.

Nyshell thought back to her toddler years. She remembered when she would waddle up and down the halls of her grandmother's house, not having a care in the world, not paying attention to anything—besides the yells. Nyshell could remember back when she could hear her grandmother screaming from the other side of the walls. She could hear her grandfather's voice booming also, barking out commands as soon as a spank would sound off. That spank would be the sound of Nyshell's grandfather's belt ripping the skin of her grandmother. Her grandmother would always tell Nyshell that she loved her granddad and that was the way love was supposed to be.

But now Nyshell realized what it was. No longer did she question the validity of her grandmother's birth marks, for they were scars. Nyshell was questioning her disposition on the matter now. She thought to herself, *Maybe this really how love is supposed to be.* She tried her hardest to get comfortable with the thought.

Nyshell sat and watched TV. Well, the TV watched her. Nyshell's phone started to ring. It was Breanna.

"You in the house?" Breanna asked.

"Yeah," Nyshell replied.

"Good because I'm at the door," she told Nyshell, so Nyshell went to open the door. "Hey, girl." Breanna hugged Nyshell. "What's wrong? You've been quiet all day." Breanna started to get comfortable.

Not wanting to mention Drew putting his hands on her, she made it short. "Drew expects for me to forget what happened because he apologized."

"When did he apologize?" Breanna asked.

"Today in school."

"What did you say?"

"Nothing. I just went along."

"Are you happy with him?" Breanna wondered.

That question made Nyshell think. It took her a minute before she finally answered. "Yeah, I'm happy." Nyshell didn't know if she was lying or telling the truth. She wanted to be happy like she was when the relationship first started.

"I love you, Shell. Don't let him be the reason for your tears." Breanna hugged Nyshell.

The tears were burning Nyshell's eyes. She knew if she blinked, they'd fall. "I love you too. So, what's been up with you and Lando?" Nyshell quickly changed the subject.

CHAPTER 9

Nyshell and Drew were back to normal. She had forgiven him and let it go. She felt that holding a grudge against him would be hurting herself.

Nyshell was in first period when Drew came in with balloons, a card, a single rose, and a single cupcake. She was caught off guard and wondering why was he bringing her those things.

"Happy anniversary, Nyshell," Drew said with a kiss on her cheek. Nyshell had forgotten all about their anniversary. "Don't tell me you forgot," Drew said.

"N-no," Nyshell stuttered. She quickly hugged him.

"Here, get your things." Drew handed over the stuff to Nyshell.

"Thank you," she said, falling for Drew all over again.

After school, Nyshell went straight home. Drew was at baseball practice, so she had nothing to do. She was on Instagram, scrolling down her timeline, when she came across a picture of Drew on his ex's page. He was smiling like everything was all good. The caption read, "My love," with the heart eyes and kissy face emojis. Nyshell's heart felt like it was about to burst out of her chest. *I thought he was at practice.*

It was the same girl from the movie theater: Keyanna. Nyshell was too humiliated to even tell Breanna what she had seen. No more than ten minutes later, people were blowing Nyshell's phone up, telling her about the picture. Nyshell wanted to comment on there, but she didn't want to look even more stupid. *I'm not coming out of character for no boy.* Nyshell was so hurt. She didn't want to believe what she was seeing. *I finally let my guard down and this is what happens? Forget this love junk. I'm too young anyway. I should've never even got involved with him.* Nyshell was heated at how stupid she felt again. *How could he? We just got back right and he goes and do this.* Nyshell's phone was ringing nonstop. She didn't want to answer, so she decided to go to sleep.

***

Breanna was up thinking about Nyshell. She had come across the picture of Drew with his ex. It looked like they were out somewhere. He had been ignoring Nyshell's calls all day. She knew Nyshell must have seen the picture because she wasn't answering and Nyshell didn't go to sleep this early. It was only 8:15, but Nyshell had forced herself to sleep.

"Get up, Shell." It was Nyshell's momma, waking her up for school.

"Ma, my stomach is hurting. Can I stay home?"

Nyshell's momma figured it was cramps, and she knew how badly cramps hurt Nyshell, so she had no problem with her staying home. "Yeah, there is some ibuprofen in the bathroom cabinet. Make sure you eat. I'm about to go to work. Love you."

"Love you too," Nyshell said, and her mom left. Nyshell's stomach wasn't hurting; her heart was. She didn't want to see Drew's face either. She just wanted to lie in bed all day.

Breanna was standing by the locker, waiting for Nyshell. Every morning, they met there. And if one of them wasn't coming to school, they would let each other know in advance. Nyshell did neither. Breanna then figured she was gonna come late, so she walked to first period.

Drew had been calling and texting Nyshell all morning, but she wasn't answering or replying. He figured she was in school, so he texted Justin and asked if she was there. Justin told him she wasn't. Then it came to him: *She must've seen the picture.*

Nyshell was lying in bed, eating cereal, when she heard a knock at the door. She got out of her bed. She heard a knock again. "Who is it?" She yelled out as she walked to the door.

"Drew."

Nyshell froze. She didn't want to open it. "What do you want, Drew?" She folded her arms and shifted her weight on one leg.

"Just open the door, baby." His voice was so sincere that Nyshell didn't even know she was opening the door until she felt a slap across her face. "How *dare* you not answer my calls? Girl, is you stupid?"

Nyshell was stuck. Drew had transformed into a whole different person. She grabbed the side of her face and stepped back.

"You don't hear me talking to you?"

Nyshell nodded her head nervously, afraid that he'd hit her again.

"Ignore my calls again and see what the hell happens!" He walked up on her until her back was against the wall. "What's up with you?" He stepped back to look her in the eyes, but she said nothing. Only tears fell as she looked at the floor. "You don't hear me, Nyshell?" He roughly grabbed her face, forcing her to look up.

"The picture," she mumbled.

"Are you serious, Nyshell?" He looked at her with a grin on his face, like it was a joke. "All this is about a picture?" He let out a chuckle.

"It's not just a picture, Drew!" she yelled.

"Lower your voice before I lower it for you." Drew was hovering over Nyshell. She was petrified. She was scared to even breathe wrong.

"Explain the picture, Drew." Nyshell crossed her arms.

"It was nothing. She and her cousin were at the restaurant also. I was with my mom."

What if he's telling the truth? Maybe I am overreacting. I'm going to ruin our relationship with these assumptions.

"I didn't do all this when I saw those pictures of you and V in your phone," he said, and Nyshell's mouth dropped. Drew peeped out at the stupid look on her face. "Yeah, you thought I didn't see?" He jacked on her arm hard.

"Ouch! You're hurting me, Drew."

"Tell me what he was doing at your house." Drew didn't let go of her arm.

V was a boy Nyshell used to talk to, but they were just friends now. "He wanted to see me," Nyshell squealed.

"Wanted to see you?" *Pop.* Drew slapped her again. "Lie again, Nyshell." He put more pressure on her arm.

"I'm not lying. I promise!" Her voice trembled. She held up her one free arm in a surrender motion.

He squeezed her arm one last time and pushed her to the floor. "Let another boy come over here and see what happens! And I don't wanna see you talking to him. Do you understand that?"

"Yes." She put her head down as tears flowed.

"I love you, Nyshell. Remember, I only act like this because I care for you," he said in his sincere voice.

Nyshell didn't know what to think. Instead of replying to him, she just nodded in agreement. She wanted to forget about the whole thing. She didn't even think it was a good idea to tell Breanna.

"Are you coming to school?" Drew put his arm around her shoulder

She flinched. Embarrassed that she flinched, Nyshell put her head down. Wanting to break down the tension in the room, she finally answered his question. "I'm not going."

"Why not?" Drew wanted to know.

"I don't feel like it. I already told my momma I wasn't coming." Nyshell crossed her arms.

"Are you coming tomorrow?"

"Yeah." Nyshell thought about how he slapped her. She was actually scared. She didn't say anything though.

"I love you, Nyshell. I really do." He gently gripped her shoulder, but she had nothing to say and sat still, staring into space. "Do you love me?" He cupped Nyshell's chin and turned her attention to him. She shook her head up and down.

Drew stayed for another hour and then left. Nyshell couldn't wait for him to go. When she got to her phone, Breanna had been blowing her phone up. Breanna was actually worried. She didn't know what to think. Nyshell sent her a text to let her know she had stayed home, but she left everything else out.

Drew called Nyshell's phone, and she picked up on the first ring. "Yeah?" Nyshell tried to sound like she was okay.

"Look, Nyshell, don't tell nobody what went on between us. That's our business," Drew said.

"You thought I was? Why would I?" Nyshell asked, unable to hide her attitude.

"Just don't. Aight?"

"Yeah, aight. I'm about to hop in the shower. I'll talk to you later." She hung up before he could even respond.

CHAPTER 10

Nyshell had forgiven Drew and everything was back to normal the next day. Nyshell was at her locker alone since Breanna said she wasn't coming. She was playing a game on her phone but stopped when she heard "Awwwws" and "Ooohhhs" coming from everybody in the hallway. She looked up to see Drew with two dozen roses and a cookie cake. "I love you, Shell" was written on the cake. Nyshell was jumping for joy in the inside. She felt like a princess.

"Are you gonna say something?" Drew laughed because Nyshell hadn't said a word.

There was a glow in her eye and her mouth was in an *O* form. She hugged him around his neck and kissed him all over his face. "Thank you, Drew. I love you so much," Nyshell said in between kisses. She never even noticed the people around laughing at her reaction. It was a very cute moment. A chapter out of a perfect love story.

"Get your cake, baby," Drew told her.

"Oh yeah." Nyshell giggled. She took the cake out of his hand. That easily, Drew had won her heart again.

***

The next day, Nyshell was walking to class when she ran into V. They talked, and he walked her to class. When she got there, Drew was already in his seat.

"Wassup, beautiful?" Drew said to Nyshell when she sat down.

"Hey, Drew." She smiled and gave him a hug.

"Warm up is on the board, Nyshell," Mr. Jenkins told her.

She nodded and started doing her warm up. She felt Drew's phone vibrate.

He checked the message and instantly grew angry with Nyshell. "Nyshell, what is this?" he gritted through teeth with his eyes on the board so he wouldn't look suspicious to the teacher.

"What are you talking about?" Nyshell asked with a confused look on her face.

"This." He turned the phone toward Nyshell. Someone had sent a picture of her and V to Drew. He was holding her books, and she was smiling at something he said. Nyshell's eyes widened out of surprise. "You don't hear me?" He started pinching Nyshell's arm.

"You're hurting me, Drew," Nyshell cried out, loud enough for other classmates to hear.

Drew put on a fake smile as he continued to pinch her arm.

"It's nothing. He only walked me to class." She tried to get away, but she didn't want to look suspicious to the teacher. "Stop it, Drew, please. You're hurting me," Nyshell begged.

"Oh, you just disrespected me and now you want me to be cool with it? I told you I don't want you talking to him!" Drew pinched harder. Nyshell wanted to scream out loud. "I better not catch you talking to him again." Drew tightened his grip on Nyshell's skin. "Do you understand what I just said?" he asked, and Nyshell nodded. "I didn't hear you." Drew made sure his grip was tight.

"Yes, Drew," Nyshell said, her voice cracking. He pinched harder and finally let go. Nyshell rubbed her arm, but it was hurting to do that. She held her other hand up for the teacher.

"Yes, Nyshell?" Mr. Jenkins stood up.

"Can I go to the restroom?"

"Yes, write a pass so I can sign it."

Nyshell wrote the pass, and Drew mugged her the whole time. Lashay noticed the looks on their faces. She began to worry about Nyshell. She knew about his violent behavior, she just never spoke on it because she was ashamed of it.

Nyshell walked straight to the last stall in the restroom and cried. She was afraid and had no one to talk to. She didn't want anybody judging her. She would tell her mom, but her mom would make her stop talking to him and Nyshell didn't want that either. She loved him too much to let him go. Nyshell cried for five minutes, then she got herself together.

"I need to go to the nurse," Nyshell said to her teacher when she walked in. Mr. Jenkins guessed that it was a girl problem, so he let her go. Nyshell went to her desk to get her stuff.

"What you need to go to the nurse for?" Drew asked with much attitude.

"My head is hurting," Nyshell replied with the same attitude. It wasn't her head; it was her heart that was hurting. She gathered her things and walked out the class.

Nyshell stayed with the nurse for the whole first period. The nurse let her lie on the hospital bed.

"Nyshell, are you going to lunch?" the nurse asked. The nurse was Breanna's cousin Vonnie.

"No, Vonnie. I'm fine but thank you," Nyshell replied.

"Well, you need to eat. I'm about to ride to McDonalds. I'll bring you something. I'm gonna lock the door, so don't open it for no one." She left and locked the door.

Breanna was sitting at the lunch table, waiting for Nyshell, who usually beat Breanna to the table. "Where's, Shell?" Breanna asked Justin when he approached the table.

"I don't know. She'll get here. Let's get in line," Justin said. They walked in the line right behind Lashay.

"Have you seen, Shell?" Breanna asked Lashay, remembering she and Nyshell were in the same first period.

"She went to the nurse," Lashay said.

"What's wrong with her?" Breanna asked herself but it was out loud.

"I'm not sure. I think Drew made her mad," Lashay answered. She knew exactly what was going on. She had seen the bruise on Nyshell's arm.

Breanna walked to the nurse's office with Justin right behind her. "Vonnie is out for lunch," Breanna said when she read the note on the door. "Where could Shell be?" Breanna asked with a confused look on her face.

"I don't know. Let's go to lunch. She'll probably be in second period," Justin said, so they walked back down to the cafeteria.

Nyshell had fallen back asleep.

"Here's your food, Shell," Vonnie said, waking Nyshell up. "After you eat, go to second period. Here is some Tylenol." She handed the food, drink, and pills to Nyshell.

"Thank you," Nyshell said.

Nyshell ate the food and took the pills, hoping the pills could do something about her headache and heartache.

Ding. Ding.

The bell rang for second period, so Nyshell gathered her things. "See you later, Vonnie, and thank you."

"You good for it, lil cuz," Vonnie put up her deuces.

Nyshell chuckled a bit, walked out, and ran right into Dejuan.

"Hey, Nyshell." Dejuan smiled.

Dang, this boy is Jim Jones' twin. "Hey, Dejuan." Nyshell smiled.

"Why aren't you in class?" Dejuan asked.

"Just came from the nurse." Nyshell tried to hide her bruised arm.

"What's wrong?" Dejuan asked with concern.

"Nothing, my head was hurting," Nyshell lied.

"You good?" He cupped her chin.

"Yes, I took a Tylenol."

"Let's get you to class then." Dejuan placed his hand under her arm, and Nyshell flinched. She put her head down in embarrassment. Dejuan took a good look at her arm and saw the bruises. Nyshell tried hiding it. "Don't let nobody mistreat you, Lil Ny. You're too beautiful." Nyshell was embarrassed, but Dejuan peeped that out. "I'm sorry to butt in, Nyshell. I should've kept my comment to myself," Dejuan sincerely apologized.

"It's okay, Dejuan. I understand."

"Let's get you to class." Dejuan wanted to change the subject. They walked in silence to Nyshell's class.

"Welp, we've reached my destination." Nyshell sighed.

"I guess so. I'll catch you later." Dejuan handed over her books and kissed her forehead.

Nyshell tried to hide her smile. "Wait, Dejuan," she called after him before he walked out the door.

"What's good, baby?" His New Orleans accent was so thick.

"Never mind." She stopped herself from asking for his number.

"What's on your mind?" He wanted to know.

"It's nothing. I'll see you later." Nyshell walked into her class.

Breanna had been waiting for Nyshell to get to class. Luckily, the teacher wasn't in there yet because that would have been

Nyshell's second write up for being late. Nyshell sat in the bleachers next to Breanna, trying her best to hide her bruises.

"Where have you been? Lashay told me you went to the nurse. Are you okay?" Breanna was worried.

"I'm good. It was just a minor headache. You want some of this drink?" Nyshell asked Breanna, purposely changing the subject.

"Yeah." Breanna got the drink out of Nyshell's hand. "You know cheerleading tryouts for basketball season are this afternoon?" Breanna reminded Nyshell.

"Yeah, I'm staying. Are you?" Nyshell asked.

"Yeah," Breanna answered.

CHAPTER 11

Nyshell and Breanna were sitting outside the school building. Nyshell usually met Drew in this spot, but he was nowhere to be found. She hadn't seen him since she'd left first period earlier.

"Oh, I forgot to tell you, Bre," Nyshell said.

"What happened?" Breanna asked.

"I ran into Dejuan before second period." Nyshell smiled.

"That's why you was late?" Breanna asked, laughing because she knew her friend.

"Yeah, he walked me to—"

Breanna slightly bowed Nyshell so that she would shut up—Drew was behind her.

"Who walked you to where?" Drew asked.

Nyshell's heartbeat sped up. "I'm talking about something old," Nyshell quickly lied.

"Um, what's good, Bre?" Drew spoke to Breanna.

Breanna nodded. She noticed how Nyshell's mood had switched up really fast. She went from herself to a frightened little kid.

"What you staying for, Nyshell?" Drew put his hands behind his back and eyed Nyshell from head to toe.

"For ch-cheerleading," Nyshell stuttered.

"Cheerleading? Your butt too fat for that little skirt," he joked but was serious.

"Shut up, Drew. They have skirts for her!" Breanna said in a joking matter.

"They better. I'd hate to have to hurt Nyshell for disrespecting me," he said, never taking his eyes off Nyshell.

"You ain't gonna do nothing to my girl. C'mon." Breanna snatched Nyshell's arm and pulled her away.

"I love to watch you walk away," Drew joked, causing Nyshell to blush and Breanna to laugh.

Tryouts went well. Nyshell and Breanna already knew they'd made the team, although they wouldn't find out until the next morning.

"Y'all did really good." Chrystal, the cheer captain, gave Breanna and Nyshell their props.

"Thanks." Breanna and Nyshell smiled.

"What grade are you guys in?" Chrystal asked.

"We're juniors," Breanna and Nyshell both answered at the same time.

"I'm a senior, so nice to meet you." She held out her hand, and they both shook it.

"Well, we have to go now. Nice meeting you. We can hang out sometimes," Breanna suggested, and Nyshell nodded in agreement. They shared their numbers with Chrystal and so did she. Chrystal was a slim girl. She had natural long hair. She was chocolate skinned with dark brown eyes. Her skin was so smooth.

Nyshell and Breanna left the gym.

"There's my momma. Text me when you get home. Love you," Breanna said.

"Okay, love you too, Bre." Nyshell waved at Breanna's mom. Breanna hopped in the car, and her momma let down the window.

"You have a ride, Shell?" Breanna's mom asked.

"Yes, ma'am." Nyshell smiled.

"Okay, love you." Breanna's mom waved.

"Love you too." Nyshell waved back, and Breanna's mom pulled off. Nyshell called her mom. Her mom said she was running late because of traffic and it would take a minute. Nyshell had no ride, so she sat and waited. She thought about calling Drew but went against it.

Nyshell had been sitting on the curb for five minutes when a black 2014 Charger pulled up.

"You look like you lost your best friend."

She'd recognize that accent anywhere. "Hey, Dejuan!" Nyshell stood.

"Why are you sitting here lonely?"

"My momma is stuck in traffic, so I have to wait for her." She had on her puppy-dog face.

"Get in. I'll take you home." Dejuan hopped out, grabbed Nyshell's books and bag, and opened the door for her. *Drew never does that*, Nyshell thought as she put on her seat belt. She shot her mom a text, telling her she got a ride. Dejuan put her stuff in the back and hopped in, and they pulled off. "What did you have to stay for?" Dejuan asked.

"Cheerleading tryouts," Nyshell answered.

"How did you do?"

"I did great," she boasted.

"That's what's up! I hope you make the team, baby." He smiled at Nyshell.

She was blushing. She loved to hear him talk, but she loved the way he said "baby" even more. "Me too," she exhaled.

The car was silent for a minute. They both were wondering what it would be like in a relationship with each other. *He probably has all types of females. We wouldn't last. He probably just wants to have sex. Then Drew would probably not let go that easy. I won't even let go that easy. I can't have both. Dejuan is a real cool dude though.* Nyshell's thoughts were all over the place.

"Nyshell?" Dejuan broke the silence.

"What's up?" She looked over at him.

"I like you. You a real cool girl. You silly, smart, and beautiful. I can't stand by and watch brah do you dirty. I won't either," he said seriously.

Nyshell only nodded. She didn't know what to say.

"I'm gonna slide by Wendy's. Do you want anything?" Dejuan asked.

"Yeah." That kind of surprised Dejuan, because other girls would try to play shy and starve themselves. They pulled up to Wendy's, and Nyshell ordered a chicken sandwich and vanilla frosty. While waiting for their food, Nyshell's phone vibrated. It was a text from Drew: *Where u at?* She was afraid to reply. Not knowing Dejuan had peeped out her facial expression, she put the phone up.

"Let me guess, that was Drew," Dejuan spoke up, and Nyshell nodded.

"Here's your food." The lady held out their food, then the drink and frosty. Dejuan nodded in a way to say "thank you," handed Nyshell her food and frosty, then pulled off.

"Thank you," Nyshell said to Dejuan.

"You good for it," Dejuan said.

The ride was silent the whole way to Nyshell's house. She was afraid of Drew's reaction to her not texting back. Dejuan was wondering how a girl so beautiful could get mistreated.

When they pulled up to Nyshell's house, Dejuan hopped out and opened the door for her. *He should've got here before Drew.* Nyshell wanted so bad to be with Dejuan, but she loved Drew so much. She felt stuck. For so long, Dejuan had been her crush, but Nyshell had figured she was not on his level. She knew she was beautiful, but she wasn't fast like the girls who threw themselves at Dejuan on the daily. Little did she know Dejuan felt she was everything he needed in a girl.

Dejuan grabbed Nyshell's things and began walking her to the door.

"Thank you for the ride, Dejuan," Nyshell said as they approached her porch.

"No problem, baby."

Nyshell turned to look at him, then quickly turned her head so he wouldn't notice her smile. She unlocked the door and sat her food on the counter.

Dejuan was feeling the living room. There was a big flat screen hanging on the wall, the living room set was black, and in the middle of the floor was a glass table on white carpet, with red, black, and silver decorations.

Nyshell's phone started ringing. "Yeah, Ma?" She put the phone on speaker and sat it on the counter.

"Do you feel like walking to get Nya from Shay's?" Shay was their cousin who lived a few blocks up from them, and since Nya was sick, she couldn't go to school, so Shay had watched her.

"Yeah, I will."

"Okay, I'll be home in another hour or so. I have a couple of things to do. Love you." Her mom blew a kiss through the phone.

"Love you too." Nyshell blew a kiss back and hung up.

Dejuan smiled, admiring their bond.

Nyshell looked over at him. "What?" Nyshell smiled awkwardly.

"I like the bond you and your mom have. That's cool." Dejuan nodded.

"Thank you." Nyshell blushed once again.

"How far does Shay live from y'all?" Dejuan asked.

"On the street before you get to the railroad tracks."

"C'mon, I'll take you."

"Are you sure? I can walk," Nyshell insisted.

"Nah, lil mama, c'mon." He walked toward the door.

Nyshell grabbed her phone, frosty, and key. Her feelings she'd had for Dejuan way back were slowly approaching without her even knowing. Dejuan opened the door and held it open for her. She locked the door, and he did the same thing when they got to the car. Nyshell got in and put on her seat belt. Dejuan hopped in the car. Nyshell watched Dejuan drive. She couldn't help but think how sexy he looked and how sexy his lips were.

Dejuan looked over at Nyshell and saw her staring. "What's up?" Dejuan wanted to know what she was thinking.

"Nothing." Nyshell looked out the window. They were already on Shay's street. "That blue house right there." Nyshell pointed at the house. He pulled up to the curb. There were toys all over the lawn. Nyshell got out, ready to see her little sister. Shay's door was open, so Nyshell walked right in.

"What's up, Shell?" Shay greeted her.

"Hey, cuz, where's Nya?"

"She's in the back, sleeping. Tell your mom I gave her some of Daquan's medicine and put her on his machine. She was coughing too badly and was stopped up," Shay informed Nyshell as they walked to Shay's room.

"Okay, thank you. How much am I supposed to give you?"

"No charge. It's all love, cuz. She's not even a problem."

"'Preciate that." Nyshell picked up Nya, and Shay handed her Nya's bags and walked them to the door.

"See y'all later. Love y'all," Shay said.

"Love you too," Nyshell said, and Shay shut the door behind them.

Dejuan was outside, talking to one of his partners. When he saw Nyshell coming down the stairs, he immediately ran to her side. He grabbed Nya and laid her on the backseat, and Nyshell put her bags in the front with her. "Imma catch you later," Dejuan told the boy. The boy nodded and walked off. Dejuan took a good look at Nya and was amazed about how much she looked like Nyshell. "Shorty is beautiful," he said to Nyshell.

"Thank you. She's a handful too. I think she has been here before," Nyshell joked. She and Dejuan laughed.

"Word, how old is she?" Dejuan asked.

"Two going on twelve," Nyshell answered. They both shared another laugh.

"That's cute." Dejuan smiled. Dejuan pulled back up to Nyshell's crib. He picked Nya up while Nyshell held Nya's bag. It would've been the perfect picture if Nya were their baby.

"You can lay her on the sofa," Nyshell told him, so Dejuan did so and walked up to Nyshell. She looked up to him shyly.

"Why you looking scared, lil mama?" He put his hands on her hips.

"I'm not," Nyshell lied. Truth was she was scared as hell. She was scared of Drew knocking on the door or him calling or something like that. Then she had that nervous feeling you get when you're around your crush. She looked up at Dejuan, and they stared into each other's eyes.

Right when Dejuan was about to kiss her, his phone rang. "Yo?" Dejuan answered. "Cool. I'm on the way now." He hung up. "That was my uncle. Imma get at you later. Here, buy you and lil mama something. Lock the door." He gave Nyshell a $50 bill and a peck on the cheek and was out the door.

She locked the door and started on her homework.

CHAPTER 12

Nyshell was excited about the cheerleading list. She knew she and Breanna had made the team, but hearing it made her even more excited.

"Wassup, Bre?" Nyshell greeted Breanna at the lunch table.

"Hey, girl." Breanna smiled at her friend.

Nyshell told her about what went on with Dejuan. Breanna thought it was okay since they were only friends. Nyshell never mentioned how they were close to kissing.

"Did you see the text about Chrystal's party this Friday?" Breanna asked.

"Yeah, I saw it."

"Do you want to go?"

"Yeah, I want to." Nyshell was excited about getting to turn up.

"And what's that on your arm? I've noticed that there have been a couple of them." Breanna eyed Nyshell's bruise.

"Oh, it's nothing. I, uh, got bit by a spider." Nyshell tried to cover it up.

"Why didn't you go to a doctor?" Breanna wasn't buying her story. She'd heard about Drew's abusive behavior. She was hoping Nyshell wasn't allowing that to go on.

Reading Breanna's expression, Nyshell spoke up, "It's not what you think, Bre. I really was bitten by a spider."

"Okay." Breanna left the subject alone, trying to give Nyshell the benefit of the doubt. "Are you excited about our first game next Tuesday?" Breanna cheerfully asked.

"Yes! I can't wait," Nyshell said halfheartedly.

"Lando said he was going to be at the party this weekend." Breanna blushed.

"Y'all are a thing now?" Nyshell smiled.

"Not quite. I like him though." Breanna sighed.

"I know that," Nyshell stated sarcastically.

***

Friday came, and the girls were party ready. Nyshell and Breanna were at Breanna's house, putting on their clothes and getting dolled up. Breanna's mom was letting her use the car tonight.

"You ready, Bre?" Nyshell asked as she looked over her outfit.

"Yeah, let's roll." Breanna gave herself a few finishing touches.

They both looked good. Nyshell was wearing light blue highway jeans, gold herrauches, and a white shirt with a gold and red rose. Her face was beat for the gods. Breanna wore skinny jeans with rips in them, a burgundy crop top, and burgundy Vans. Her face, too, was beat for the gods.

When Nyshell and Breanna arrived at the party, everybody from school was there. Nyshell was glad she agreed to go to the party because she needed to clear her head. Boys were asking them for dances and trying to holler at them, but they turned them down. All the boys at the party were trying to get dances from the big booty girls, except for Dejuan and Lando. Breanna spotted them while they were sitting on the sofa near the kitchen, laughing and joking.

"Come on, let's go over there with my man," Breanna joked.

"Girl, you see Dejuan back there. You know Drew would kill me," Nyshell said in a voice of a frightened little girl.

"Oh, so Drew can do whatever he wants, but you can't? I think not. You're coming back there with me," Breanna demanded.

"Okay, I guess," Nyshell said. At first, Nyshell was nervous because it was risky for her to be in public with Dejuan, but she figured since Drew felt it was okay to be on Instagram with his ex, she could have an innocent conversation. As Nyshell and Breanna walked over to Dejuan and Lando, Nyshell's nervousness turned into happiness once she saw Dejuan smile. It was like when she saw Dejuan, all her worries went away. Their vibe was always perfect.

"Come on, baby, let's go to the party room," Lando said to Breanna. They both got up and walked toward the party. As they walked off, Nyshell yelled, "You think you're slick, Lando!" He acted like he didn't know what she was talking about and laughed.

"What's wrong? You can't be right here by yourself?" Dejuan asked, wanting her to tell the truth.

"It's not that. I just don't know . . ." Nyshell hesitated.

Nyshell and Dejuan made small talk for a few seconds. He was a nice guy, and she wanted him as much as he wanted her, it was just that she was in love with Drew. They sat in awkward silence until Dejuan said, "I heard you made the cheerleading team. Congratulations."

"Yeah. Not to be cocky, but it was pretty easy," Nyshell boasted.

Dejuan laughed and said, "Well since you're so good, I'll be at your games, if that's okay with you."

"You sure you're not going to be there for the other girls?" Nyshell joked, knowing Dejuan could get any girl on the cheerleading team.

They laughed as Dejuan said, "Still got jokes, I see. It's cool."

For a minute, Nyshell had forgotten about everything, even Drew, until she saw him through the crowd of people. Nyshell's whole demeanor changed and Dejuan sensed it.

"What's wrong, ma?" Dejuan asked, concerned, looking through the crowd. When he saw Drew, he knew. Nyshell was quiet. "I'm not trying to get you in trouble, so I'll just get up," Dejuan said. As Dejuan was getting up, Drew walked over.

Drew hovered over Nyshell as she sat on the sofa. Dejuan just stood there to see what was about to happen. He knew something wasn't right with them. The way Nyshell's demeanor changed when she saw Drew—she acted as if she was afraid of him. Dejuan was trying to figure out in his head if the day that he walked her to class, Drew hit her since he had no problem putting his hands on her that day at the theater. He figured it would be rude to ask, so he didn't. He did know one thing for sure: Drew wasn't about to hit her while he was right there. Dejuan pulled his phone out and sat on the edge of the sofa, as if he wasn't listening.

"You're really trying my patience. Trying to make me look like a fool, aren't you?" Drew said through clenched teeth.

Nyshell tried to explain. "Drew, I'm not—"

"Shut up!" Drew demanded, cutting her off as she got silent. Dejuan wanted to say something so bad, but he knew it wasn't his place. "Get up, we're about to go," Drew demanded, leaving no room for questions.

Dejuan stepped in. "You don't have to leave if you don't want to."

"Who asked you?" Drew said, irritated.

Dejuan replied, "You didn't have to."

Not wanting any commotion, Nyshell quickly said, "I'll go."

Dejuan didn't say anything, knowing regardless of what he said, she was going to leave. He wanted to protect her from Drew, but he knew that it would be a waste of time. As she walked off, Dejuan looked at her with disappointment.

Nyshell was scared for her life. Even if she had stayed with Dejuan, she couldn't run from Drew forever. Actually, staying would've only made things worse. Drew walked through the party with his arm around Nyshell's shoulders, as if nothing was wrong. When they passed Breanna and Lando, Nyshell stopped to tell Breanna she was leaving. Nyshell looked normal, but Breanna knew something was wrong.

"You can't leave without me, remember? Your stuff is at my house," Breanna lied, thinking Drew might do something to Shell.

"Oh yeah, and you're my ride."

"She's just going to step outside with me," Drew said.

Breanna just agreed and left it alone.

Being outside with Drew didn't make Nyshell feel any better because no one would be outside with them. He could do whatever he wanted to her. As they walked out the front door, she wanted to scream for Dejuan to rescue her.

As soon as Shell and Drew were outside, he snatched her by her shirt, he pulled her to his mom's car, forced her in, and got in as well. "You think I'm stupid, huh? You're at this party with your little boyfriend and then going to call me tonight like it's all good?" Drew might as well have been talking to himself because Nyshell was too scared to answer. "Answer me!" Drew yelled as he smacked Nyshell across the face.

Nyshell burst into tears as she held her face.

Drew grabbed her hair, turned her head toward him, and said, "I don't care about your tears. Start talking—now!"

Nyshell started explaining through tears, "I don't have anything going on with him. He's just a friend."

Drew was livid, so he didn't hear anything. He grabbed her neck, looked her in the eyes, and said, "So now you're going to lie to me?"

"I'm not lying!" Nyshell said, raising her voice, which only made Drew throw punches at her as she put her hands up to block her face. The punches kept coming, and Nyshell finally started punching back. Nyshell knew how to fight, but the strength of a man was no match for her. Drew also had a couple of inches of arm's reach over her. They were seriously brawling.

Nyshell finally opened the car door and jumped out to run back to the party. Drew jumped out as well. As soon as she turned the corner, Drew on her heels, she ran into Breanna, Lando, and Dejuan. A safe feeling came over her. It was evident all over Nyshell's face that she had been fighting. Nyshell's face was wet with sweat, her shirt was a little ripped, her lips and nose were bleeding, and her hair wasn't as good looking it was before she came outside with Drew. Breanna, Lando, and Dejuan were all shocked, their mouths dropping.

Seeing Nyshell look beaten up outraged Dejuan. "You can fight a girl, fight me," Dejuan said as he and Lando walked toward Drew.

"NO!" Nyshell jumped between the two. Nyshell was embarrassed that the commotion was about her.

After the boys calmed down, Breanna decided it was time for them all to go. Drew walked off without saying anything to Nyshell. He just gave her a look that gave her chills. Nyshell dropped her head to avoid eye contact. She asked Breanna for the car keys so she could sit in the car. When she got to the car, she laid back in the passenger's seat, closed her eyes, and started thinking about everything: Drew, Dejuan, the embarrassment, and what would be next.

While she sat in the car, Breanna, Lando and Dejuan stood outside, talking about everything that had happened. Dejuan decided to leave Lando and Breanna alone. He could've gone and sat in his car, but instead, he walked to Breanna's car. He wanted to check on Nyshell to make sure she was good. "Knock, knock," Dejuan said as he knocked on the car window, causing Nyshell to jump.

"You scared me," Nyshell said, giving him a small grin and causing him to smile back.

"Roll down the window," he said, and Nyshell did as he said, politely asking what he wanted. "I just came over here to check on you after the way everything—" Dejuan started to explain.

Nyshell interrupted, "Yeah, I know." She was embarrassed and didn't want to talk about it.

Dejuan, getting the message, put his hands up in a surrender motion and said, "Just take my number. Call if you need anything." He walked off just as Breanna was walking up. Dejuan and Breanna said their goodbyes and hugged.

When Breanna got in the car, Nyshell was hoping Breanna wouldn't say anything, even though she knew Breanna would. Nyshell asked to get dropped off at home. She wanted to be alone. Breanna understood, so she did so.

Nyshell went straight to her room and cried. She was too embarrassed to say anything to anyone. She cried and cried. She wanted to know what she was doing wrong to make him so angry toward her. She felt so bad for even talking to Dejuan. She regretted the minute she had walked over to him.

Breanna and Nyshell met up that Saturday to hang out. They were coming from Joe's Crab Shack. The whole time, Nyshell was distant. Breanna wanted so bad to ask, but she didn't want Nyshell to feel offended. Never being the one to hold her tongue, Breanna finally spoke up. "What's with you and Drew?"

Nyshell responded, "I rather not talk about it."

"Well, I want to talk about it," Breanna protested.

Nyshell didn't say anything. Out of nowhere, Nyshell got a text and started smiling.

Breanna smiled. "Is that Dejuan?"

"No, it's Drew," Nyshell responded, as if Breanna was going to jump for joy.

Breanna gave Nyshell a look that could kill as she pulled over. "Are you freaking kidding me?" she yelled as she snatched Nyshell's phone to read the message. When Breanna read the messages, she became more than livid. "He just apologizes, and you forgive him? Just like that? He'll never change if it's that easy," Breanna angrily yelled.

"People make mistakes, Bre. You act like you're just perfect," Nyshell said in Drew's defense.

"I never said I was. I know one thing, I'm not abusive like your crazy cheating boyfriend is," Breanna shot back.

"If you really were a good friend, you wouldn't judge my decisions," Nyshell yelled.

"So now I'm not a good friend? I'm trying to paint the picture clear for your little brain to understand. I'm the one you call when everything happens. I'm the one who always has to cheer you up. I'm the one that tries to help you while no one else cares. You're just too stupid and naive for Drew to notice. So, if that's how you feel, then oh well. Find someone else who'll put up with you." Breanna was talking with her hands.

"Fine!" Nyshell nonchalantly responded.

It was a good thing that Breanna was pulling up in front of Nyshell's house because the awkward silence would've killed them both. When Nyshell got out, she slammed the door. Breanna pulled off before Nyshell's foot even made it all the way in her yard.

Breanna's feelings were hurt that Nyshell just responded with "fine." She felt like Nyshell had chosen Drew over her. This argument wasn't like any other where they just make up right after.

CHAPTER 13

Nyshell and Breanna didn't text the whole weekend. Nyshell was secretly hoping that Breanna would text her, but she never did. They both were stubborn, but this time, Nyshell had crossed the line. Nyshell knew she had said some things she shouldn't have, but she felt like Breanna was judging her. In Nyshell's eyes, she had the right to talk to whomever she wanted, without Breanna judging her.

Nyshell and Drew were back on good terms, so he spent the whole weekend at her house. Saturday, Nyshell's mom took Nya to a birthday party and left Drew and Nyshell alone almost all day. Nyshell was lying under Drew with her pants down, getting ready to have sex.

"Can I try it without the condom?" Drew asked.

Afraid of making him mad, she said yes. *One time wouldn't hurt*, she thought. Nyshell, being naive and in love, didn't see much wrong with it, as long as he pulled out. She felt like many people used the method and nothing happened, so she figured she wasn't any different. She was also curious about how it would feel. This was one of her biggest mistakes.

***

Nyshell was standing at her locker when Justin walked up and asked where Breanna was. Nyshell shrugged, said she didn't know, and walked off, which made Justin wonder what had happened with them. He figured it was just some petty girl drama and decided to stay out of it. When Justin ran into Breanna at lunch, he noticed that Nyshell wasn't with Breanna, but he didn't bring up the subject because he didn't want to seem messy.

Nyshell and Breanna had avoided each other all day at school until the period after lunch, gym. In gym, they were doing a drug and alcohol awareness poster and were partners. Breanna was sitting in the bleachers, texting, while their teacher was taking attendance, and then in walked Nyshell, right after the bell sounded. Breanna wondered why Nyshell was late, but her pride wouldn't let her talk to Nyshell, who walked right past Breanna and sat a couple of rows above her. Breanna moved over to where she could see Nyshell, because no matter how long they'd been friends, Breanna still wasn't about to let anyone she didn't like sit behind her. Nyshell saw Breanna scoot over and knew that the argument was deeper; she knew Breanna was big on the whole "never turn your back on an enemy" thing. It kind of hurt Nyshell's feelings because she felt like she and Breanna would never be enemies, even if they were arguing. Nyshell felt like if Breanna thought they were enemies, she would too. As soon as the teacher told everyone to get their posters, Nyshell went over to the teacher and told him that she and Breanna had decided to work separately. It was petty, but Nyshell didn't care. She was trying to get back at Breanna, but to her surprise, when Breanna found out, she didn't even look Nyshell's way. Breanna was being the bigger person.

When class was over, Chrystal was waiting on Nyshell and Breanna at the door. Breanna left first. "Hold on, Bre," Chrystal said while waiting for Nyshell to come out. Once Nyshell came out the door, Chrystal told them, "We were going to introduce the new cheerleaders at the party Friday, but you guys were nowhere to be found."

"Something came up," Breanna answered for the both of them and then got quiet.

Nyshell stood quietly, thinking about the night of the party.

"Oh okay." Chrystal said awkwardly because of the silence.

"Well, see you later," Nyshell spoke up as they all walked off.

Chrystal didn't know if the girls were trying to be smart or not, but she definitely knew that there were some bad vibes. She thought they were being shady toward her, but she just brushed it off.

After school, Nyshell and Drew walked pass Breanna and Lando, who seemed happy as they were walking hand in hand to Lando's car. Nyshell noticed that Lando opened the car door for Breanna. It made her kind of jealous because she and Drew had been dating longer, but Drew never opened the door for her. "Drew, why don't you open the door for me?" Nyshell asked sincerely.

"Don't start," Drew stated sternly, so Nyshell dropped the subject, not wanting to upset Drew before they got to the house. Drew had his mom's car, so they didn't have to catch the bus home.

On the way home, they stopped at the corner store to get a couple of snacks. While they were in the store, in walked Dejuan. Nyshell was afraid to even look his way while Drew was there. She felt Dejuan looking at her, but she refused to turn her head. She felt bad, but she knew Drew was watching her. When she got to the counter to pay for her things, Drew was still trying to decide what he wanted. Nyshell placed two bags of Ruffles, a brownie, and a Sprite on the counter.

The man said, "$3.06."

Just as Nyshell was pulling the money out of her pocket, Dejuan stepped to the counter and said, "You'll never have to pay for anything as long as I'm around." He pulled a crisp $20 bill out of his pocket and placed it on the counter.

Nyshell quickly rejected the money and put her own money on the counter. $3.06 exactly. If Drew weren't in the store, she would've let Dejuan pay, but she didn't want to disrespect Drew.

Drew stepped to the counter where Dejuan was and said, "She's good."

Dejuan laughed and put one hand up in surrender while he pointed to the $20 sitting on the counter with the other, telling Nyshell she could have it.

When Dejuan left the store, Nyshell reached for the money, but Drew smacked her hand, as if she were a little child about to touch a hot stove. "Are you serious?" Drew asked, shocked that Nyshell was about to take the money.

"What? I'm not just going to leave it sitting there," Nyshell replied, but Drew snatched the money, balled it up, and threw it on the floor as he pulled Nyshell out of the store by her collar. "Drew, let me go!" Nyshell screamed, but Drew was ignoring her as he threw her into the car.

Dejuan was still in the parking lot, sitting in his car, but when he saw Drew handling Nyshell, he quickly got out and walked toward Drew's car. "Aye, man, I'm not about to watch you put your hands on her like that," Dejuan said seriously, clearly not caring about Drew being a little bit larger than he was.

"Then don't watch," Drew said, clenching his jaw as he walked around to get in his car.

Nyshell was, yet again, embarrassed in front of Dejuan. She didn't want Dejuan to feel like he had to rescue her.

As soon as Drew pulled off, he started yelling at Nyshell like she was his child. "You think I'm stupid!" Drew kept saying. Nyshell just sat and listened, hoping that her mom was home. "So now you can't answer me?" Drew yelled as he pulled the car over. Before Nyshell could say anything, Drew said, "Get out."

Nyshell was baffled. She responded, "No, I'll get out after you take me home."

But Drew wasn't trying to hear anything Nyshell was saying or about to say. He got out of the car. Nyshell knew he was about to come to her side, so she locked the door, not realizing that he had the key in his hand. He unlocked her door and pulled her out of the car as she kicked and held on to the door. Drivers passing by blew their horns as a signal to tell Drew to stop, but he didn't care. Nyshell put up a fight for a good minute until Drew slapped her so hard that she froze. The slap stung her cheek and eye. He jumped back in the car and pulled off.

Nyshell sat on the sidewalk, wishing that they would've stopped at the store by her house. She couldn't believe that Drew had put her out of the car like that. She didn't even feel like she had disrespected him. She sat there thinking for a while, then figured that throwing herself a pity party wasn't going to solve anything. Her house was a twenty-minute walk she didn't want to take. It was hot, and she was exhausted. She didn't want to call her mom because she knew that her mom would ask questions. Suddenly, Dejuan popped in her head. She quickly pulled her phone out of her bag to call him. As the phone rang, she secretly hoped Dejuan wouldn't answer. She was tired of being embarrassed in front of him. It felt like his phone rang forever. As soon as she was about to hang up, she heard him say, "Wassup?"

"Um, hey, Dejuan, it's Nyshell," she replied hesitantly.

"Oh, what's wrong?" he asked.

"Can I have a ride?" she asked, getting straight to the point.

"Yeah, where you at?" Dejuan said, as if it were no problem. She explained to him where she was and was surprised that he didn't ask any questions. Dejuan pulled up about three minutes later.

When Nyshell got in the car, the AC and the radio were on. She was grateful for the music, because when music was playing, no one was talking. When no one was talking, no questions were being asked. At least, not aloud. Nyshell could see all over Dejuan's face that he had a million questions. When they pulled up at the red light, Dejuan reached to turn the music down. The radio being turned off was Nyshell's biggest fear at the moment. She loudly said, "Let the questions begin."

"What?" Dejuan said, confused at what Nyshell was talking about.

"I know you're about to ask me some questions," Nyshell said.

Dejuan replied, "Actually, I wasn't. I just figured the music was too loud for you."

Nyshell didn't notice she was making faces. Nyshell was embarrassed. "I'm sorry."

"You don't have to be. You're good," Dejuan genuinely said. The car grew silent, and it stayed that way for the rest of the ride to her house. As Nyshell was about to open the car door, Dejuan said, "Listen. I'm not trying to be all in your business, but what you allow will continue."

"I thought you wasn't trying to be in my business," Nyshell snapped.

"I'm not." Dejuan said, not trying to argue with her.

"Thanks, Dejuan," Nyshell sincerely said as she got out of the car, but Dejuan just sat quietly. He waited for her to get in the house, then drove off. When Nyshell got in the house, a message came to her phone. She thought it was Drew, but it wasn't. It was Dejuan. The message read, *You might want to consider wearing makeup tomorrow.* It also had the smiley face emoji. Dejuan was being smart. Nyshell didn't get what he was saying. She texted him back and asked him what he meant, but she got no reply. She thought he was calling her ugly until she went into the bathroom and realized that Drew had bruised her face.

When Dejuan got home, Lando was already there. He didn't know Breanna was there until he went into Lando's room. He went in there to talk to Lando but decided that he should tell Breanna instead. Dejuan told the two that he was thinking about fighting Drew but realized he shouldn't after Breanna told him what happened after they left the party. Dejuan had a dilemma and didn't know what to do. After Nyshell had tried to snap on him today, he decided to just fall back.

Nyshell knew that she was going to need help covering the bruise, so she decided to figure out a lie to tell her mom before she asked what happened. A volleyball accident in gym was the best she could think of. As soon as her mom got home with Nya, Nyshell decided to say something about her face before her mom did so it wouldn't seem suspicious. As her mom walked in the house, Nyshell called from the bathroom, "Ma, can you come here and look at my face?"

When her mom walked in the bathroom, she gasped at the bruise that was now purple. "What happened? Did you get into another fight?" her mom asked with concern.

Nyshell had told her mom she was into a fight the day Drew beat her up. "No, I got hit in the face with a volleyball today," Nyshell lied.

Her mom didn't question it because she didn't suspect Nyshell to lie to her face, so she thought nothing of it. "You're so clumsy.

We're going to have to use a little makeup to cover that up," Nyshell's mom said as she went to get some makeup. "You have to be more careful, Shell," her mom told her as she placed makeup on the part of her face that had turned colors. When her mom was done, Nyshell thanked her and told her that she would be more careful.

Nyshell sat around watching TV as she waited for Drew to text, like he did all the time. To her surprise, he didn't text or call at all. At ten o'clock, she decided to try to call him. It rang three times, then he sent her to voicemail. She thought maybe he was tired, so she just decided to go to sleep.

When she woke up the next morning, she still didn't have a text or a call from Drew, so she decided to text him and apologize about the whole store incident. He still didn't reply. She decided to go on with her morning. She got ready and caught the school bus.

Breanna had called Justin the night before to tell him about Nyshell's bruise that Dejuan had told her about. Just because she and Nyshell wasn't getting along didn't mean she didn't care about her. Breanna knew that Justin wasn't a punk and that he didn't play about either of them, so instead of letting Dejuan say something, she thought it was best to let Justin do something about it since he and Drew were close friends.

Justin and Breanna were standing in the hall when Drew walked past. Justin walked up to Drew and aggressively asked, "Wassup with you putting your hands on Shell?"

Drew tried to brush Justin off but couldn't because people were in the hall and had heard Justin check him. Drew replied by saying, "She's mine, and it's none of your business." Drew sized Justin up.

"Let me make this clear: if you ever put your hands on Nyshell again, it's going to be a problem."

Drew smiled and smartly replied with a "Whatever." Justin was cool, but Justin wasn't anybody to play with.

Justin and Drew had drawn a crowd, so before anything could even go down, principal Jones was in the hallway clearing it out. Justin and Drew were still standing up on each other. "Is there a problem?" the principal asked.

Drew smirked and answered, "Nah."

Justin just stood there with his mug as Drew walked off.

"Get to class!" Principal Jones yelled as Justin and Breanna walked off.

When Drew walked into first period, Nyshell was already sitting down. It was evident that he was upset about something. Nyshell thought that he was still upset about what happened yesterday, so she decided not to say anything. Drew didn't sit next to her in class or look at her the whole class period.

Nosey Lashay leaned over to Nyshell and asked, "Did you hear about Justin and Drew about to fight in the hall?" Nyshell looked confused, but before Nyshell could say anything, Lashay answered for her, "Guess not, but it was about you."

As soon as Nyshell was about to ask questions, the teacher looked at her, telling her to be quiet.

When first period was over, Drew stood outside the door, waiting for Nyshell to leave the class. As soon as she walked out, he grabbed her arm as he pulled her toward the lockers. Nyshell was wincing in pain because he was also pinching her while looking her in the eyes. He noticed the makeup under her eye and on her cheek. Through clenched teeth, Drew said, "Don't you ever send anybody to check me again."

"I—" Nyshell tried explaining, but Drew walked off on her. Nyshell was furious but not at Drew. She walked down the hall, the opposite way of her class, so she could find Justin. While she was searching for Justin, she ran into Chrystal, who was telling her that they had practice after school at four. "Yeah, okay I'll be there," Nyshell responded. She quickly brushed Chrystal off to find Justin. When she ran into Justin, he and Breanna were talking in the hall. They stopped talking when Nyshell walked up with her mad face. Nyshell looked at Justin. "Who told you to say anything to Drew about me?" Nyshell asked, trying to check Justin.

"I did," Justin answered, not caring about Nyshell being mad.

"Well, I didn't. I'm tired of y'all always in my business. Justin, mind your own business with your little girlfriends. I don't be—"

Justin cut her off. "Don't worry about it again. I ain't fooling with you anymore. You on your own." He and Breanna walked off while Nyshell stormed off in the other direction. Justin shook his head as he and Breanna walked to class. "She'll learn one day," he said.

"Hopefully," Breanna answered.

CHAPTER 14

Nyshell and her team were getting ready for the basketball game. The gym was live and waiting for the players.

"You all sit here and look pretty until the basketball players come out," Nyshell's coach said excitedly. She was so ready to see her girls perform. Nyshell was happy to give the crowd a show. This was their third game. She looked around the gym to see who all she knew. She saw a lot of familiar faces, but only one stood out. Dejuan was posted on the wall. He was wearing a Green Bay Packers vest, a black long-sleeve shirt, black jeans, and black boots. His gear was always tight. Nyshell felt that funny feeling in her heart that she always gets when she sees Dejuan. It was the same feeling she used to get with Drew, but she hadn't felt that for him in a while.

Nyshell hadn't spoken to Dejuan since she'd gone off on him. She felt that she owed him an apology. Nyshell thought up a quick lie to tell her coach so she could apologize to Dejuan. "Coach, can I please run to the restroom? It's gonna be quick." She put her hands in the prayer form.

"Yes, Nyshell, hurry back." The coach eyed Nyshell. Nyshell, Breanna, and the coach had a great bond, considering the fact that she was friends with both of their moms.

Nyshell walked over to Dejuan. "Hey, Dejuan, can I have a word with you?" she softly asked.

"Yeah, sure." He followed Nyshell outside the gym.

Breanna watched the two and silently hoped that Drew wasn't seeing them. Just when she thought about it, she saw Drew watching Nyshell and Dejuan leave the gym. She saw him shake his head and head back downstairs. Drew had come upstairs to get a good luck kiss from his girl. Breanna wanted to give Nyshell a heads up, but her coach was on them about leaving. She decided to stay and just wait for Nyshell.

Nyshell and Dejuan walked as far as possible for privacy before she said anything. "I wanted to apologize about the way I acted toward you. I was just so mad and irritated at the moment. I feel so bad for treating you that way when all you wanted to do was help," Nyshell confessed with her head almost in her lap.

"It's cool." Dejuan was short about it. He then began to walk off.

"Wait, Dejuan," Nyshell called after him, and he gave her a look that said, "What?" "Never mind." She waved him off, feeling stupid to think he'd just forgive her.

"I told you you can speak your mind. Now, what is it, Nyshell?" He began to soften up.

"No, it's just that . . ." She paused to find the right words.

"Just what?" Dejuan wondered.

"I like you, Dejuan." She sighed. "I really do. It just seems as though I can't get rid of him. I'm really in love with him. I wish I could make things right. When I was crushing on you, you weren't even paying attention to me. I feel stuck. I know Drew hitting on me isn't right, but he promised me he'd stop." Nyshell started to tear up.

"C'mon, lil mama. Don't start crying. I'm not pressuring you to be with me. I just want better for you. I don't like seeing you being mistreated. You so beautiful. And plus, I don't want to feel like a rebound. Be with a person because you want to be with that person. You just have to open your eyes. To know love, you have to know if it's really love or not. Love is happiness. Be happy, lil mama. That's all I want. The bruises and crying have to stop. All that is up to you though." Dejuan had said a mouthful, but it was exactly what she needed.

Not knowing what to say, she just came out and said something, "Thanks for agreeing to talk to me. I needed it." She hugged Dejuan and didn't want to let go. She felt so safe and stress-free with him.

"The game is about to start. Let's get you ready, cheerleader," Dejuan swung Nyshell around, causing her to giggle like a little kid. Suddenly, she felt this strange urge to throw up and went to the nearest door she could find.

"Nyshell, are you okay?" Dejuan pulled her hair back from in front of her face.

"Yeah, I've been feeling a little sick all day. It's nothing." She brushed it off.

"Shell!" Breanna called her name. "Coach is looking for you. The players are coming out in a minute. Wassup, Dejuan!" Breanna approached the two and gave Dejuan a hug.

"I'm coming, Nyshell stubbornly stated. She was being petty. "I'll catch you later, Dejuan." Nyshell gave him a hug and walked off. Breanna followed behind. It slipped Breanna's mind to tell Nyshell that Drew saw her and Dejuan walk out. The two got back just in time.

"What took you so long?" Coach side-eyed Nyshell.

"I was throwing up." Nyshell grabbed a bottle of water.

"Are you okay? You want to sit out for first quarter?" Coach grew with concern.

"Nah, I'm cool." Nyshell finished the bottle of water and grabbed her pompoms. The cheerleaders lined up as the whole basketball team ran through the line with pompoms being shaken all over them. Drew was the last to come out. He gave Nyshell the look of death. It made the hairs on her neck stand right up. She quickly looked at the floor to avoid eye contact. Breanna picked up what was happening. Just when she remembered to tell Nyshell that Drew saw her, Coach interrupted.

"Come on, ladies. Line up. Bre, you call the first cheer, then Chrystal, then Nyshell. Taylor, you call the fourth one," she said as she looked at her clipboard.

Breanna kicked herself for not remembering to tell Nyshell when she went to go get her.

The first and second quarter went by with Drew and his team being in the lead. It was halftime, and the teams were headed to the locker room. Nyshell was headed to the concession stand.

"C'mere," Drew gritted through his teeth. He walked her to the girls' locker room. Nyshell was petrified. The minute they were out of everyone's sight, he started to get rough. He was almost dragging Nyshell. He roughly pushed her inside the locker room.

"What I do, Drew?" Nyshell pleaded as she began to take steps back.

"You think I didn't see you and Dejuan?" Drew took steps forward.

Nyshell's mouth dropped. "No, I can explain." She backed up to the lockers.

"Explain what?" He backhanded Nyshell, causing her head to slam against the locker. Her lip instantly burst and tears flooded her face.

"Please don't do this, Drew. I have to go back out and cheer," Nyshell begged and sobbed.

"Don't do what? What I tell you about disrespecting me?" He yanked her by the hair and hit her in the face continuously.

She tried getting him off her, but it was no use. He was so much stronger than she was. The hits were hurting but not as much as they did when he first started abusing her. Sadly, she was getting used to it.

"You gonna learn to respect me." Drew pushed Nyshell on the floor, making her hit her leg.

"Ouch!" she winced in pain. She tried getting up but couldn't, then Drew left the locker room. Nyshell felt so miserable lying there. She didn't even want to get up off the floor.

Drew headed back upstairs. Breanna saw him come out of the double doors, and that's when she noticed Nyshell wasn't around. She went to the concession stand and the restrooms, asked people had they seen her, then decided to head downstairs. "Nyshell!" Breanna yelled through the hall.

Nyshell could hear Breanna, but she was afraid to say anything. She knew Breanna's temper.

"Nyshell!" Breanna called for her again. This time, her voice was closer, but Nyshell decided to say nothing. Breanna walked in the locker room, and her heart exploded at the sight of Nyshell balled up in the fetal position with tears coming out of her eyes. Her lip was bleeding, and there was a big bruise above her knee. "Oh my God!" Breanna rushed to Nyshell's side. It crushed her heart to see her best friend that way. "What happened to you, Ny?" Breanna's eyes watered.

"I fell down those stairs right there," Nyshell lied.

Breanna knew it was a lie. She just brushed it off, not wanting to start an argument about Nyshell's abusive boyfriend. "Let's get you upstairs." Breanna helped Nyshell up.

Nyshell wrapped her left arm around Breanna's neck, and they slowly walked upstairs.

"What happened?" Coach asked when she saw Nyshell. She and all the other cheerleaders rushed to her side to help. Nyshell told her the same lie. Coach believed her. She called Nyshell's mom to come and get her. Coach told Nyshell's mom she would be back to normal the next day and not to worry. All the while, Drew watched, feeling no remorse for what he had done.

Nyshell was afraid her mom would question her about it when they got home, but she didn't. She gave Nyshell some ice and Tylenol. Nyshell went up to her room and flopped on the bed. She didn't even bother to turn on the TV. She just replayed the beating. She asked herself if she really loved Drew and answered, *Yes.* She wondered if Drew really loved her. She thought about the conversation with Dejuan. *He was right,* she thought. It pained her to admit it, but she had no choice.

Nyshell drowned in her own tears. Her heart was aching. Then there was this sharp pain in her stomach. The pain went on and on until she forced herself to sleep.

CHAPTER 15

It took three days for Nyshell's leg to get better. Her bruise went down only a little, but that didn't stop her from going to practice. After her last class ended, she headed straight to the gym. She would usually stand outside, but she had no one to stand outside with. She and Justin hadn't spoken to each other since the argument, and she wasn't sure if Breanna had forgiven her or was just being a good friend last night. For the first time, Nyshell felt alone. They were her only true friends, and she had let a boy come between them—a boy whom Nyshell loved dearly but also the boy who had tried to break Nyshell down time after time. Nyshell knew that what she was going through with Drew wasn't right, but she loved him and felt obligated to stay with him.

While Nyshell sat in the gym with her earphones in, listening to Pandora, she couldn't help but think about herself and Drew. The other teammates arrived, interrupting her thoughts. As everyone walked in, Breanna and Lando showed up. Nyshell noticed that Lando was holding Breanna's bags. She thought, *Drew never holds my bags.* Seeing Lando and Breanna made Nyshell kind of jealous. She wanted the same type of love she felt that Lando gave Breanna. Nyshell was starting to realize that she deserved better than Drew.

Her thoughts about Drew ended as Chrystal snatched her earphones out of her ears to tell her that practice was about to start. Nyshell placed her phone down and went to the warm up circle. The mats were down, so everyone knew that they were going to be practicing flying. As practice went on, Nyshell began to feel dizzy. She decided it wasn't anything and shook the feeling off. Nyshell, Kate, Terri, and Mia were spotting for Breanna when Nyshell's nauseous feeling came again. Nyshell turned around just as Breanna was coming down. Breanna would've hit her head if it weren't for Kate quickly taking up Nyshell's slack.

When Breanna got on her feet, she was furious. She couldn't believe that her best friend would do that to her. Breanna went straight after Nyshell, wanting to fight.

Before Breanna could catch up to her, Kate had grabbed Breanna's arm, trying to explain what had gone down. "It wasn't even like that," Kate said.

Breanna didn't want to hear anything. She just wanted to kill Nyshell. By the time Breanna had gotten to the hall, Nyshell was gone. Breanna turned around to go back in the gym. Coach was asking Breanna what had happened. Breanna told their coach that Nyshell had purposely tried to drop her. Breanna wasn't being evil, but she seriously thought that Nyshell had intentionally done it. Coach ordered Breanna to go home early to cool down while she went to find Nyshell to tell her that she was suspended. There was zero tolerance for hurting team members.

Once Nyshell heard the news, she stormed into the gym, grabbed her things, and walked out. Her mom wasn't expecting her to get out of practice until 7:00, so she was nowhere around. Nyshell was about to catch the bus when Dejuan pulled up. It seemed as if Dejuan always showed up in her times of need. He was just about to leave school, so he rolled his window down and offered her a ride.

She accepted it. The car ride was silent until Nyshell finally spoke, "You must have known I was going to get kicked out of practice, huh?" she sarcastically asked.

"Kicked out of practice? How does a Goody Two-shoes get kicked out of practice?" Dejuan jokingly laughed.

Nyshell laughed back and replied, "Whatever, it's a long story."

"We got time," Dejuan replied. On the way home, Nyshell told Dejuan everything that was going on. How she and Drew weren't on good terms, how she had no friends. It seemed as if everything had just been relieved of her when she talked to Dejuan. On the inside, Nyshell kind of felt selfish because she never asked Dejuan what was going on in his life, mainly because she was scared of what he'd say.

It was evident that Dejuan and Lando were in some type of illegal thing. People just didn't know if it was selling drugs, faking checks, or robbing. While others wanted badly to find out, Nyshell wanted to stay as far away as possible. She only wanted to see the good in Dejuan. And that's exactly what he'd shown her, so the rest didn't matter. Dejuan was Nyshell's relief. He didn't judge her, and that's exactly what she needed in her life at the moment. Everybody was always telling her what she should and shouldn't do, but Dejuan just listened. On the way home, they stopped at Louisiana Seafood to get something to eat.

"$30.56," the cashier said, reading the total of Nyshell and Dejuan's food. Dejuan started to pull the money out like it was nothing when Nyshell volunteered to pay half.

"Put your money up. I told you as long as I'm around, you don't have to pay for anything."

"I just don't want you to think I'm using you," Nyshell replied back truthfully.

"Nah, ma, I know for a fact that ain't the case," Dejuan said, smiling, and Nyshell smiled back.

They picked a table and started eating. They had so much food they couldn't eat it all. They left and decided to go to the movies. Nyshell didn't want to go in her practice clothes, but Dejuan made her feel like it didn't matter, so she decided to go anyway.

"What movie do you want to see?" Dejuan asked.

"I've really been wanting to see *Run All Night*, but we can see what you want," Nyshell said, not wanting to seem pushy.

"Nah, it's cool. I'll watch that."

Nyshell and Dejuan were standing in line to receive their tickets when Nyshell, out of nowhere, turned around and threw up. Everybody was looking at her with pity, some disgust, while Dejuan tried to help her. Nyshell had thrown up all over her clothes. She felt like her insides were coming up. He walked Nyshell back to the car and told her to stay inside. He drove around to H&M, and Nyshell gave him her size.

"Lock the doors," Drew said before getting out.

When he came back, Nyshell was slumped over in the seat, looking like she was about to fall asleep. Nyshell thanked him and took the bag of clothes. When Nyshell was changing clothes, she was surprised that Dejuan didn't even try to look at her. He just waited for her until she was done. She liked the outfit her bought her. He bought her blue jeans with rips in them that are known as "boyfriend" jeans. He also bought a white blouse that said "text him maybe"—Nyshell found that cute.

Dejuan cut the music off to respect her while she was asleep. Dejuan was a gentleman, and Nyshell loved that about him. Dejuan's phone rang, waking Nyshell. Her eyes were still closed, but she was listening. "Wassup? Nah, I'm busy right now," she heard Dejuan saying. With her not being able to hear the other person, she didn't know who it was.

When Dejuan hung up the phone, Nyshell asked, "Oh, you're busy with me? I feel special." Nyshell smiled at him.

Dejuan laughed. "You should always feel special," Dejuan honestly said, with no intent to offend Nyshell.

Those words cut her deep, though, because Drew always made her feel like garbage. Dejuan, on the other hand, treated her like a princess, but she was in love with Drew. Nyshell was starting to feel like a damsel in distress. Dejuan always saved her. He stopped at the store and got Nyshell some ginger ale and crackers. He returned to the car and handed the bag to her.

"I don't feel bad anymore, but thank you," Nyshell said as she passed the items back to Dejuan.

"You still need to at least eat the crackers," Dejuan said, giving the crackers back.

This time, Nyshell kept them. "I think I ate some bad food," Nyshell said, and Dejuan agreed. Nyshell changed the subject, "Let's go to your house."

"You sure?" Dejuan asked, and Nyshell nodded her head yes. Dejuan pulled off and went right past what Nyshell thought was Dejuan's house.

"Where are you taking me?" Nyshell asked.

"You said you wanted to come to my house," Dejuan said.

"I thought you lived in the blue house," Nyshell said, confused.

"A lot of people think that," Dejuan said. They rode for about five minutes until they reached a subdivision. The houses were about twice the size of the ones in Nyshell's neighborhood. They finally pulled into a driveway, and Nyshell quickly recognized Lando's car. As they got out, Dejuan told Nyshell not to be nervous.

"What do I have to be nervous about?" Nyshell asked, scared of what Dejuan would say.

He replied back, "Nothing. That's why I told you not to be nervous."

When they walked through the door, a short light-skinned lady came up and greeted Nyshell. She quickly realized that the lady was Lando's mom. They looked just alike, but she was just a shade lighter than Lando. He introduced them to each other, and they clicked right away.

"It's about time you brought a girl home," Lando's mom joked.

"Nah, Ma, we just friends," Dejuan replied back.

Why did he call her "Ma"? I thought he and Lando were cousins. Nyshell was confused. "Um," she said as his mom walked away.

"Come on," Dejuan said as Nyshell followed behind. Dejuan walked Nyshell away from all the noise into some type of game room. No one was in there but Lando.

"Wassup, Lando?" Nyshell greeted.

"Good to finally see you over here," Lando replied with a smirk.

"Whatever." she laughed. Nyshell finally had thought to charge her phone. As soon as she cut it on, she had seventeen messages from her mom and Drew. Nyshell didn't realize that it was past ten. "I have to get home now!" she quickly told Dejuan.

Dejuan grabbed his keys without a word once he heard the urgency in Nyshell's voice. He sped to Nyshell's house through a silent car ride. Once he pulled up, he asked her if she wanted him to go talk to her mom, but she declined.

As soon as Nyshell walked through the door, all hell broke loose. Her mom was in the living room, and it was clear that she was livid. Before Nyshell could even explain herself, her mom was charging at her like a bull who saw red.

"Why didn't you let anybody know you were going to be home late? We were worried about you. And then I find out that you're suspended from the cheerleading team for dropping Bre!"

Nyshell was just silent as her mom went on and on. She knew that saying something would only make it worse. Nyshell wasn't a confrontational person. She'd rather just sit quiet until the yelling stops.

"Say something!" her mom yelled with rage.

"I forgot," Nyshell timidly answered.

"That's all you can say? Just forget it. You're off the team, and you're on punishment. Don't leave my house," her mom said, ending the whole conversation.

Nyshell just walked to her room and decided to text Drew. She knew he was going to be mad, but she had to get it over with. He didn't text back, and Nyshell figured that he was too mad because he was always mad at her. She just decided to give him space instead of texting multiple times. Nyshell turned on the TV to watch *Love and Hip Hop*, then she got a message. She thought it was from Drew, but to her surprise, it was from Dejuan. She was confused because Dejuan had never texted her with a conversation. Surprisingly, she was happy that he'd texted her. She was starting to like Dejuan more and more. She felt guilty, but she was realizing that maybe Drew was no good. Drew was abusive and messed with other girls. Dejuan, on the other hand, was kind and honest. She was stuck between the one she loved and the one she liked.

She and Dejuan ended up talking on the phone all night. Dejuan even convinced Nyshell to text Breanna and tell her what happened. She explained to Breanna what really happened and apologized. Breanna also apologized for overreacting.

When Nyshell woke up in the morning, her phone was still counting. Nyshell and Dejuan had fallen asleep on the phone.

She put her ear to the phone and smiled as she heard Dejuan breathing. Nyshell finally hung the phone up and went to brush her teeth. Her mom walked in the bathroom to get some tissue. It was awkward because of the conversation last night. The two of them never made eye contact.

About five minutes later, Nyshell heard the front door lock and the car door slam. She didn't know where her mom had gone, but she knew she'd left. Nyshell started feeling really sick all of a sudden. She rushed to the toilet and threw up. Then there were the cramps she's been feeling. Nyshell was throwing up a lot lately, but she never stopped to think about it. She then looked at her period calendar.

Nyshell was three weeks late. "This can't be true." Nyshell put her hand over her mouth. She started pacing back and forth. Nyshell didn't want to believe what she was thinking. "I can't be," she repeated to herself over and over. She was trying to remember when she and Drew had had unprotected sex. She agreed to doing it only one time.

Nyshell was afraid of talking to Drew. She hadn't spoken with him since the game. Nyshell cried and cried. She contemplated calling Breanna but was afraid of what Breanna would say. She finally decided to. The phone rang three times before she hung up, regretting that she even called. The phone rang within a minute, causing Nyshell to jump. Nyshell answered but said nothing.

"Hello!" Breanna's voice was loud as usual.

"He-hey, Bre," Nyshell uttered.

Breanna could sense something was wrong with her longtime best friend. "What's wrong, Ny?" Breanna asked with concern.

"Nothing," Nyshell tried lying. She had to laugh at herself for even trying that with Breanna.

"Come on, Ny, I was born at night but not last night," Breanna said with her mouth twisted and an eye roll.

Nyshell didn't want to talk about it over the phone, so she asked Breanna to come over. It took no time for Breanna to get to Nyshell. She was knocking on the door in less than ten minutes. When Nyshell opened the door, it was evident to Breanna that Nyshell had been crying. As soon as Breanna walked in, Nyshell broke down, crying. Breanna was crying too and didn't know why. She was just hurt seeing her best friend hurt. For a moment, she didn't want to know why Nyshell was so upset; she just wanted to comfort her. She rocked Nyshell back and forth while rubbing her back. After what it felt like hours of crying, Nyshell finally calmed down.

"Look at you." Nyshell laughed at Breanna as they both wiped their faces. "You don't even know why you're crying, crybaby," she teased on.

"So, leave me alone and tell me what's going on." Breanna flicked Nyshell off.

Nyshell explained to Breanna how she believed she was pregnant. She brought up the incidents of her throwing up and having morning sickness.

Breanna couldn't believe it. "Have you mentioned it to Drew?" Breanna asked.

"No, I don't know how to say it. What if he overreacts?"

"And by overreact you mean hit you?" This made Nyshell's mouth drop. Seeing Nyshell's reaction, Breanna went on to say, "Yeah, you think I don't know?" Breanna crossed her arms. Nyshell said nothing. "Why do you put up with him and his baggage?" She honestly wanted to know.

"I love him so much. I want things to go back how they were in the beginning. It was like a perfect love story. Now it's imperfect and broken. I know he loves me. He just has a hard way of showing it. He will realize one day." Nyshell was trying to convince herself more than she was Breanna.

"By then you'll probably be dead and he'll be in jail because of this 'perfect love story' you're trying to put together." Breanna's words cut Nyshell very deep. She began to tear up, knowing what Breanna was saying was true. Breanna couldn't put it any other way and didn't want to. She wanted Nyshell to wake up and smell the coffee.

Nyshell thought back to the day of her grandmother's funeral.

Nyshell was only six years young. She was riding in a black limousine along with the rest of the family. She was sitting next to her mom, who was wearing all black with big dark shades. Nyshell was wearing a black sundress, a black blazer, and black flats, and her hair was in a big bun. She was looking at everyone around her crying and was wondering what was wrong. Nobody ever said anything. The car stopped in front of a church, the one her grandmother attended. She silently wished her grandmother were here to get her mom to stop crying.

The family walked inside the church. Nyshell walked alongside her mom down the middle aisle of the church. They finally reached a stopping point in front of a lady who looked so much like her grandmother. She then looked around to see if she could see her grandpa. He was nowhere to be found.

"Why is my grandma lying here, Mommy?" Nyshell looked up to her crying mother, but her mom said nothing. She could only stare at Nyshell. "Where is Papa?" Nyshell needed some type of understanding, but her mom stayed quiet.

After the funeral, the family went to a place Nyshell remembered as the grass with stones in it. She still didn't see her grandfather. Nyshell's mother fainted when her mom was put into the ground.

Chills went down Nyshell's spine as she thought about what had really happened. Her grandmother had lost her life to the man she loved. Nyshell remembered sneaking and reading the letters her grandpa had written to her mom. Her mom had never replied to him. She acted as if she didn't even have a father.

"So, what are we going to do?" Breanna asked, taking Nyshell out of her daze.

"I need to take a pregnancy test." Nyshell leaned back on the couch.

"How are we going to get it?"

Nyshell shook her head. "I don't even know."

CHAPTER 16

Breanna called and asked Lando to take them to the nearest store. Nyshell was scared of Dejuan finding out, so she was hesitant. She tried to act as normal as possible. Lando pulled up to the CVS. Nyshell and Breanna hurriedly walked into the store. They looked around for pregnancy tests for about three minutes before finding them.

"Which one do we get?" Breanna asked as if she was taking one as well.

"I don't know. This one says we'll find out right after," Nyshell said as she read the box. She picked up two tests and went to pay for them. Nyshell was so embarrassed when paying for the tests.

Back at home, Breanna and Nyshell were in the bathroom, reading the instructions.

"Ok, so just pee in this tube and squeeze it on the test. If the line appears and is red or even light red, you're pregnant," Breanna explained, so Nyshell grabbed the test and began pulling her pants down. "Don't piss on your hand, Ny," Breanna said with disgust as she watched Nyshell.

"Nothing is going inside the tube," Nyshell informed Breanna. Nyshell washed herself. "Hold this." She tried giving the tube to Breanna.

"No, your piss on that!" Breanna yelled at Nyshell. They both burst out laughing.

Nyshell didn't do the first test right and the second test fell in the toilet, so she decided to try it another time.

The next day, Nyshell was looking around for Drew. She wanted to tell him what was going on, but Breanna walked up, holding her purse really close and tight.

"What you carrying? A gun?" Nyshell joked, making both of them laugh.

"Follow me." Breanna grabbed Nyshell's hand and guided her to the restroom no one ever really went to. They went into the last stall, which was the biggest one. "Here." Breanna handed Nyshell a pregnancy test. After leaving Nyshell's house yesterday, Breanna had stopped and bought another one.

Nyshell took the test, and this time, she did it right. They waited a minute, which felt like an hour, for the results to show. The line appeared as red. Nyshell's mouth dropped and tears fell from her eyes. She couldn't believe it. Although she suspected it, seeing it was different.

Breanna couldn't believe it either. She was scared like it was herself. "So what? We have to figure something out." Breanna tried getting Nyshell to think straight.

"I can't," Nyshell repeated to herself over and over. She seemed possessed. Breanna shook Nyshell, but all she kept saying was "I can't." It was scaring Breanna. Then the bell rang. "I'll see you after first period," Nyshell said to Breanna, who was trying to figure Nyshell out. Nyshell had this crazed look in her eyes.

Nyshell walked to first period. Drew was sitting in the seat next to Nyshell's. Nyshell sat and said nothing. Drew picked up on how Nyshell was acting, but he said nothing either.

Later that day, Drew went to Nyshell's house. "What's going on?" Drew asked Nyshell as soon as she opened the door. She said nothing, so he asked again.

"I'm pregnant, Drew." Nyshell's head was in her lap.

"Well, I can't have no baby. I have sports to worry about. So, what are you going to do?"

She couldn't believe what she was hearing. Her heart broke into a million pieces. Nyshell tried holding her tears.

"It's probably not mine anyway. Go tell Dejuan. I don't want nothing to do with you or a baby," Drew said and walked out of Nyshell's house.

Nyshell didn't even chase him. She had already made up her mind what she was going to do.

CHAPTER 17

Nyshell was at home and lying on her bed. Breanna was texting her phone constantly, trying to see what was going on, but Nyshell didn't reply. She shut her phone off and went to get some water.

Nyshell was burning a hole in the floor as she paced back and forth, contemplating her next move. "I can do it," Nyshell stated over and over, trying to convince herself. "Stop acting like a punk. It's going to be quick." She kept on talking. She was trying hard to decide what she was going to do.

Nyshell was too afraid to tell her mom what she was going to do. She was thinking her mom wouldn't accept her after finding out. She was stuck. After going back and forth, she finally made her decision. "Here it goes." Nyshell swallowed the pills. She started feeling very dizzy and fell backward on the bed.

Everything went black.

Thanks for your support!

Marilyn S.